THINE ENEMY

THINE ENEMY

by

RALPH W. NEIGHBOUR

Author of *A Voice From Heaven* and
The Shining Light

)))7

ZONDERVAN PUBLISHING HOUSE
GRAND RAPIDS, MICHIGAN

To

RUTH

My faithful helpmeet in the service of the Lord

THINE ENEMY

Therefore if thine enemy hunger, feed him; if he thirst, give him to drink: for in so doing thou shalt heap coals of fire on his head.

Be not overcome of evil, but overcome evil with good. Romans 12:20, 21

CHAPTER 1

REX BRANTFORD PREACHED A SOUL-STIRRING MESsage to his new congregation at his initial morning service, the last Sunday of May. He chose as his text, Romans, chapter twelve, verses twenty and twenty-one, "Therefore if thine enemy hunger, feed him; if he thirst, give him to drink: for in so doing thou shalt heap coals of fire on his head.

"Be not overcome of evil, but overcome evil with good."

A fresh, cool, morning breeze made fragrant by pine trees, blew gently into the valley where the little white church was situated. The laughing waters of a crystal-clear, gurgling creek meandered aimlessly through the valley below the church. The quiet serenity of the spot was delightfully enticing, inviting worshipers to leave the turmoil of the outside world to seek the peace it afforded.

All nature seemed to chant an amen to the morning message, whispering, "God is love." The scenic beauty of the Allegheny Mountains in north central Pennsylvania, where the Radford Community church was located, exceeded the architectural grandeur of the world's most fabulous cathedral.

Rex Brantford, middle-aged, about six feet tall, affable and gentle in speech, was meticulously dressed in a black suit. His upright stance and athletic appearance indicated he was not one to be pushed around, and yet his friendly countenance intimated that he could be approached both by sinners and righteous alike. Smiles of contentment wreathed the faces of the worshipers, indicating their complete satisfaction with their new shepherd.

If it was true that the people were sizing up their new pastor, it was equally true that the pastor was appraising his new congregation. He was most favorably impressed with the sincerity and open-faced honesty of the people of the congregation who appeared to cling to his every word. *These are a rugged people,* he thought, *individualists, who enjoy the simplicities of life, unspoiled by the synthetic materialism of city life.*

9

Rex noticed that they were cautiously scrutinizing his wife, Blanche, who sat near the window overlooking the valley below. She had purposely dressed in her most reserved spring clothes to avoid antagonizing these plain people, but her natural beauty could not be concealed. Her deep brown eyes spoke sweetness, and her flawless, soft complexion proclaimed her gentleness and culture. When she arose to sing, people couldn't help but notice her graceful, lithe, slim body which reminded them of an artist's painting of spring.

Blanche appeared to be lost in a trance as she dreamily gazed through the window toward the church graveyard, which reminded those who worshiped how near they walked by the threshold of eternity. The tombstones seemed to cry, "Prepare to meet thy God."

Rex and Blanche had come to share both the sorrows and joys of these people, whatever might betide them. The plain sanctuary of the church was not too impressive, but only the people were important. However, the golden oak altar rail, matching pews, pulpit, communion table and pulpit chairs, were in keeping with the rugged character of these mountaineers. The auditorium was not luxurious, but it was orderly, clean, and well kept.

Blanche shook her head approvingly whenever Rex drove home an extremely important truth. Her eyes smiled upon him.

"Christianity is essentially love; therefore, if we do not love our enemies, we have missed the very purpose of Christianity," he said.

"Christianity is sheer mockery if we fail to forgive those who do evil against us."

The congregation appeared to agree, and an occasional amen expressed their enthusiasm. Neither Rex nor Blanche dreamed that hate smoldered within the hearts of some of these people.

After the benediction, the new pastor stood at the door to shake hands with the people as they departed. They were warm in their felicitations and enthusiastically welcomed both the pastor and his wife to their new parish.

A peaceful serenity was settling over the soul of Rex, until Deacon Amos Wadsworth shook his hand with such a vice-like grip that he cringed with pain. A smile that dripped honey labeled the deacon in Rex's mind as being hypocritical.

"That's real preaching, Pastor," Deacon Wadsworth said. "Keep that up and you'll pack out this church. That's exactly the kind of preaching we need. I've always said that if a preacher isn't afraid to preach the truth, the blessing of the Lord will rest upon him. I like a preacher who hits me right between the eyes, and you surely did just that this morning."

Rex's eyes narrowed and his face sobered as he sized up the deacon. He had a long, wrinkled face and was dressed in a seedy, almost threadbare and years outdated suit. His long-tailed coat was on the verge of being ridiculous. Obviously, he was bent on making an impression, desirous that people should consider him to be a man of great importance and weight.

You'll bear watching, Rex thought. *I hope I don't have trouble with you.*

The majority who received the new pastor and wife that morning, were most gracious, but one other person stood out like a tree fallen across a highway, namely, Maggie Streetland.

Maggie brushed by Blanche and hastened to meet the new pastor. She was dressed in expensive but ill fitting clothes. Her speech was affected and unnatural; her posture was commanding and domineering. Rex's impression of her was instant and final: domineering, extremely emotional and insanely egotistical.

Obviously, this woman has an inferiority complex, he thought. *Her chief interest is in herself. Her clothing indicates an insatiable thirst to be accepted and liked.*

"Pastor," she said affectedly, "I want you to know that I'm going to stand by you, and with my help we will convert this whole valley to Christ. I'll be your assistant pastor, so to speak, and if ever you need my help, I'll be the one person upon whom you may depend."

She's dangerous, Rex thought. *I'll do all in my power to understand her and, at the same time, I'll be careful not to cross her if possible. Poor thing, she's obviously abnormal.*

Rex shook her hand warmly and said cautiously, "Thank you, Mrs. Streetland, you are most gracious. I'll remember your kind offer."

Maggie stalked out of the church, but suddenly returned. Brushing by everyone at the entrance she sought out Blanche. Her frozen face suddenly melted and she became quite loquacious.

"I just met your lovely daughter, Charlene, outside the church. I think she's a dear . . . such a lovely girl . . . and has the sweetest face . . . looks just like her mother, doesn't she? How old is she? No . . . don't tell me; let me guess . . . now, let's see, I'd say about sixteen. Am I right? Didn't I hit it just about on the head? Such soft blue eyes and lovely golden hair . . . she'd make a perfect match for my son . . . they were just made for each other and . . .

and . . . say, wouldn't it be a joke if they really did make up to each other and got married some day? Ha, ha, ha . . . I'd be the happiest person on earth if that happened, wouldn't you?"

Blanche's countenance froze and hidden horror crept into her eyes. "Why, yes, that is, it would be a surprise, now wouldn't it?" she answered.

Other women, who had been talking with Blanche, withdrew as soon as Maggie Streetland appeared. They seemed to resent her, or else they feared her. Blanche wasn't quite sure which was true.

It was almost one o'clock before Rex and Blanche finally left the church to go to their car for the drive to the parsonage, about one mile up the valley. Charlene was impatiently waiting for them in the Chevrolet. Just as Rex started to drive away, the Sunday school superintendent, Sam Leighton, came running to the car.

"Pastor," he said, "I don't like to delay you, but would you mind talking privately with me, in the church office, for just a few moments? It's most important, and I feel you should know about it immediately." Turning to Blanche and Charlene, he apologized, "You'll forgive me, won't you?"

"Certainly," Rex agreed as he stepped from the car. "I won't be long," he said to Blanche, "but if you wish, you may drive on home and Charlene can return for me."

"We'll wait," Blanche said.

"Now," Rex sighed when they reached the pastor's study, "what seems to be the trouble?"

"It's about Mrs. Maggie Streetland's son, Gary. He's our Sunday school treasurer, and he has stolen almost fifty dollars of Sunday school funds. Seems he had a chance to fly to Philadelphia with a pilot who happened to make an emergency landing at the airport near here, last week, and the temptation was too great, so he stole the money from the treasury to make the trip. The boy has always been crazy about airplanes, but he never before had a chance to fly, and he was so determined to go, he didn't stop to consider the consequences."

"How old is Gary Streetland?" Rex asked.

"Just eighteen. He's a senior in high school. He's a great big bruiser, weighs about two hundred pounds, I'd say. Looks a lot like his mother."

"Can't he pay the money back if we give him time and opportunity to do so?"

"I doubt it; he's never worked a day in his life. Look, Pastor, the boy's to be pitied. I don't want to sound critical, but the truth is, his mother has browbeaten him since he was a kid. She's a domineering sort of person, therefore, Gary doesn't have any self-confidence, so he hasn't ever earned a dime since he was born, and if his mother ever finds out that he stole that money, she'll beat the daylights out of him."

"That's too bad, but don't you think his mother would pay back the stolen money if she were informed about it? Or doesn't she have the money?"

"To hear her talk, she's got scads of money, but sometimes I wonder if it isn't all bluff."

"Well, tell me, is Mr. Streetland living? I wasn't introduced to him in church this morning, so I was wondering about him; is he dead, or doesn't he attend church?"

"Gary's step-father is alive; his father died a few years ago. Guess he got tired of living with that woman, and that was the only way out. 'Course, I shouldn't say that, but it's so, anyway. The step-father is sort of a mouse who never says much and never goes anywhere; Maggie talks and goes enough for the whole family."

"I'll call Gary to my office first thing tomorrow afternoon, as soon as he's out of school," Rex said. "We'll try to straighten out this affair in such a way the boy's reputation won't be hurt, and I agree we shouldn't tell his mother anything about it."

"Thank you, Pastor."

"And thank you, Brother Leighton. I want you to always feel free to come to me with any problems that may arise. God sent me here to share your burdens."

Both Blanche and Charlene waited impatiently for an explanation from Rex after he returned to the car, but he didn't say a word until they were almost home.

"Well?" Blanche queried.

"Well, what?" Rex answered.

"You know what. Don't keep us in suspense. What happened?"

"Oh! I was just thinking it over. It's a little personal problem regarding Maggie Streetland's son, Gary. It'll work out all right, I'm sure, with the help of the Lord."

"Oh-h-h! You mean that drip, Gary? I just met him," Charlene sighed. "What a nightmare to a girl's dreams! I'd sooner die an old maid than marry a baboon like him."

"Charlene!" Blanche exclaimed. "I'm ashamed of you. I never

thought you'd ever talk about anyone like that, and you call yourself a Christian. You don't sound like my little girl."

"Oh, well, I might as well say it as think it, hadn't I? I
wouldn't have disliked him so if his busybody mother hadn't introduced him to me and insisted that we were the perfect match and
almost had us married on the spot. I just can't stomach him, but I
do feel sorry for him, having the mother he does. She'd drive any
kid crazy."

Rex's eyes twinkled and he grinned as he winked at Blanche,
who returned his look knowingly. Neither of them commented
further on what Charlene had said, for they couldn't sincerely blame
her for feeling the way she did about Gary and his mother.

Finally, Rex broke the silence by saying, "Isn't this beautiful
country? I think we'll love it here. How about it, Charlene?"

"I already love it," she said. "Daddy, do you think there are
any trout in that stream?"

"I'm sure there are. We'll have to give it a try, won't we?
Think you could catch a trout?"

"I'd sure like to try. Will you show me how, Daddy?"

"It's a deal! Well, here we are at our new home. What a
paradise! All we need do is step out of the back door and it's
as if we were in the Garden of Eden! I was told that, in the fall,
I could see deer by sitting on the back porch and watching the
mountainside. The deer graze there during the early morning."

"Daddy, someone told me the grouse are so plentiful, they fly
up in coveys of two and four at a time, but it takes an awfully
fast shot to get one. I wish you'd get me a twenty gauge shotgun
so I could hunt. Of course, I wouldn't be able to hit one, but I
could maybe scare them to death."

Blanche grinned. "You stop making a tomboy out of my little
girl," she scolded.

"I'm no little girl," Charlene objected. "I'm eighteen and
plenty able to take care of myself."

"Maggie Streetland thinks you're sixteen, and I let her keep
on thinking it."

"That's an insult; I haven't been sixteen for two years now,
and that's a long time."

"Well, let's quit the arguing and get some dinner on the table,"
Rex said. "This mountain air surely gives me an appetite; I'm almost starved to death."

"You don't need any mountain air to give you an appetite,"

Blanche quipped. "How about helping me in the kitchen while Charlene sets the table, and we'll get dinner ready sooner?"

Rex had been careful not to discuss the people of the church in Charlene's presence, for he had made it a rule never to share the burdens of his ministry with her, lest she might become discouraged in her Christian life, but as soon as he and Blanche were alone in the kitchen, he asked, "Well, what do you think of our new church? That is, the people?"

"Oh, I just love them," Blanche said sincerely. "They're wonderful! So sincere, simple, honest and kind . . . absolutely unspoiled. I just love them all to death. They're the kind who will come to us with their troubles, just like children run to their parents. Makes one really want to help them."

"I feel the same way," Rex said. "There are only two in the whole church whom I fear, Maggie Streetland and Deacon Wadsworth. I size him up as being as treacherous as a viper, and she's a sick girl, very sick, and therefore extremely dangerous. We must handle her with kid gloves and be careful never to cross her if possible. She needs our help in the worst kind of a way, but if she ever turns against us, we'll need God's help, for she could become violent. We must always keep that in mind and exercise great care to avoid injuring her ego. She's sick but exceedingly shrewd and capable, and though people naturally withdraw from her (I noticed that in church this morning), nevertheless, she could lead them astray, for they would not know how to cope with her. They are not her equal in sagacity and cunning. In fact, she's a speckled bird, far above the average person in this valley, socially, intellectually, financially, and in experience."

Blanche stood motionless beside the stove, lost in deep thought. "Isn't it strange how you and I always size up people in about the same way? Everything you've said about these two people, I've already thought. Incidentally, it's a good thing I'm not the jealous type."

"Why?"

"Did you see how Maggie brushed me off and devoted all of her charm to you? I was just a stumbling block in her road." Blanche laughed.

"At least you don't need to be jealous of her," Rex said. "Poor thing, she is so offensive, and yet she is so in love with herself. That's the reason she is what she is; it's a reaction against her frustration in trying to be important, thus bringing forth her strong ego. She's to be pitied, yes, to be pitied."

"Just so the situation remains that way, so she's the one to be pitied and not us. I'm afraid the tables may turn."

"So am I," Rex said. "Let's just hope for the best."

"You can put the meat and potatoes on the dining room table," Blanche said, "I'll have the gravy made in just a minute."

Each one prayed before eating, Charlene first, then Blanche, and finally Rex.

"Aren't you glad we came here?" Rex asked. "Surely the Lord's been good to us."

"Yes," Blanche agreed. "We have so much for which to be thankful, we should be most charitable to others in return for His goodness."

Before they had finished eating, one of the members of the church interrupted their meal by bringing some fresh eggs and a country ham. "Thought you might enjoy having a good breakfast," he said. "We ain't got much money, but we'll shore see to it that you have plenty to eat."

After dinner, the three of them sat in the swing on the front porch, drinking in the fresh air, listening to the cheery song of the birds, and relaxing in the solitude of the mountain quietness.

"This is the nearest thing to heaven," Rex sighed. "I don't think there could ever be any violence here. It's so quiet and peaceful."

Another car drove up, and this member brought them a gallon of maple syrup, also a large bag of buckwheat flour, "just so's you can have a good, hearty breakfast."

It looked as if breakfast were the only meal that counted until Mrs. Bazemore, a widow, brought them a big fat hen, "which is the best for stewing there is."

The evening service was as gratifying as the morning, for the little church was filled to capacity, which proved that it was the center of social life in the valley where there was neither television nor other competitive entertainment. Six responded and came forward when an invitation was extended for those who wished to accept Christ as their Saviour.

Only one thorn discomfited Rex, namely the prospect of dealing with Gary, whom he had not yet contacted. *I'll make an appointment with him after the service,* he thought.

For some inexplicable reason, however, Gary slipped through the crowd and out the front door before Rex could speak to him.

"Gary," he called after him, "could I see you before you leave?"

"Yeah? What for?" Gary questioned skeptically.

"Something personal and private," Rex said. "I'll be through greeting the people in a few moments if you don't mind waiting."

"Okay," was Gary's blunt answer.

After the crowd had left, Rex found Gary waiting outside the church and said, "Gary, would it be convenient for you to meet me in the church office after school tomorrow afternoon? There's something I'm anxious to discuss with you."

Gary shrugged his big, round shoulders nonchalantly, grinned sheepishly, disguised his sourness with an expression of indifference, and said, "Okay," before he turned and slouched away.

Rex watched him disappear in the darkness. "Reminds me of a big bear," he murmured as he observed his huge build and lumbering walk, hands always in his pockets. "That boy is rebelling against society for some reason, and I wonder if it isn't a reaction against his mother's dominance?"

CHAPTER 2

HIGH SCHOOL HAD ALREADY DISMISSED WHEN REX drove by on his way to the church office, and young people were exploding with the pent-up energy which had accumulated during the past six hours. Slowing down, he searched the crowd of young people for Gary, so he could drive him to the office, but he couldn't find him, therefore he drove on.

After waiting at the office for nearly an hour, he put on his hat and was just preparing to leave the office when Gary lumbered in.

"Come in, come in," Rex invited cordially. "I had almost given up hope that you were coming and was preparing to leave."

"Yeah. I had to stay in," was his brief explanation.

Gary took a quick glance at Rex, then looked at the floor, unable to meet the pastor's gaze. As usual, his hands were in his pockets and he shifted nervously, jerking his right shoulder and changing his weight from one foot to the other. He appeared to have two left feet and two left hands. He wore a heavy wool knit sweater.

"Sit down, sit down," Rex invited. "My, but you're a husky fellow, just the kind of timber they're looking for on the football team. You do play football, don't you, Gary?"

"Naw."

"I suppose you go in for outdoor sports, Gary? I would imagine you're the type of fellow who likes hunting and fishing. Right?"

Gary warmed up just a little bit and a faint, winsome smile broke upon his face. Immediately, Rex saw a side to Gary he hadn't thought existed. He yearned to help him somehow. *It's too bad*, he thought, *this lad has been spoiled by his mother, and though his potential for good is great, if something doesn't change present trends, he's doomed.*

Gary chanced to glance up for a moment at Rex, then dropped his gaze to the floor again, "Yeah, that's right. That's me. I like to hunt and fish and we're never without venison at my house. Me and Dad go spotting deer at night with a flashlight. There's plenty of speckled trout in the creek back of the house, too, and we always get our share one way or another, if not by hook, by crook."

Rex raised an eyebrow, but knew better than to inquire further into the illegal sports activities of Gary and his father . . . not at this particular time, at least. That could wait for a later date after the present difficulty had been straightened out and Gary's confidence had been won. However, Rex began to understand even more why Gary was what he was and feared for his future more than ever.

Rex approached the problem at hand cautiously, saying, "Gary, I understand you're the treasurer of our Sunday school. Is that right?"

"Yeah, I'm treasurer."

Gary stiffened and became extremely nervous. His eyes shifted back and forth and his mouth twitched nervously. His face grew red; and he arose and backed toward the door.

"Sit down, sit down, Gary," Rex insisted. "I want you to know, I'm glad you're our treasurer and, believe me, we appreciate the work you're doing for the Lord in this capacity."

Gary looked up inquiringly, searching Rex's countenance to make sure of his sincerity. He slumped back into his chair and gazed at the floor again.

"I might as well get right to the point, Gary. The Sunday school superintendent spoke to me yesterday regarding the shortage in the Sunday school funds. I thought . . ."

"Are you accusing me of stealing?" Gary demanded. His entire attitude suddenly changed from timidity to aggressiveness.

Anger fed his courage until he was able to look Rex in the eye. He became as restless as a treed cat at bay.

"No, Gary, I'm not accusing you of anything; I'm merely offering to assist you in straightening out any misunderstanding which may exist, for I do not wish to condemn you, nor to hurt you, but rather to help you. Understand? I'm sure there's some reasonable explanation for what has happened, and I'd like to hear your side of it."

"Well, well . . . I — I . . . imagine they got their reports all mixed up, and . . . and . . . they're trying to blame it all on me. I'm not going to take no more from them either; I'll just resign and you can get someone else to do the dirty work."

"But Gary, that wouldn't solve the problem at all. We must clear you, regardless. Now tell me, just how much is the Sunday school fund short, and how did it happen?"

Gary jumped to his feet, clenched his fists, trembled with rage, and stared at Rex with inflamed eyes. Rex was astounded at Gary's complete transformation. He had suddenly become another character, aggressively dangerous. "Reverend," he shouted, and then his voice choked with anger, "don't you dare accuse me of stealing. I warn you! I'll not stand for it, and neither will my mother. I'm going to tell her how you've tried to frame me, and when she hears about it, there'll be trouble, plenty. You'll regret having accused me."

"Gary, sit down," Rex spoke sternly. "There's no reason for you to become so upset. I'm not accusing you of stealing, nor trying to harm you in any way. Believe me, I'm only trying to help you."

Gary sat down, breathing heavily, and again stared at the floor.

"Now," Rex said, "let's talk this thing over sensibly. There's a certain responsibility goes with every office which we can't escape, and in this case, you're treasurer of the Sunday school, and . . ."

"I'm not any more! I quit!"

"All right, so you quit, but that doesn't change the fact that we must balance the account before the books are turned over to your successor. Right?"

"I 'spose so."

"Of course. Now, Gary, there's only one way this thing can be straightened out and I want to help you to do it. Would you be willing to go to the Sunday school superintendent, Mr. Leighton, and compare your books with his weekly offering envelopes to discover what, if any, discrepancy exists? I'm sure that when the two of you get together, you'll be able to iron out the difficulties, and I'd personally appreciate it if you would put forth an effort to come to an

agreeable understanding with Mr. Leighton. We don't want this
thing to get out of hand, for it might hurt both you and the entire
church. We wouldn't want that to happen, would we, Gary?"

Gary knew perfectly well that the Sunday school superintendent would prove him guilty. It was one thing to deceive a new
pastor who didn't know him, but quite another thing to fool the
Sunday school superintendent who both knew his past record and
also possessed incriminating evidence in proof of his guilt. Nor
was he willing to admit his defection. Gary had never confessed a
fault in his entire lifetime to anyone.

"Reverend Brantford," Gary raised his voice and pounded
his fist on the desk, "you can have your old Sunday school treasury
job. I told you, I'm through! I've quit, so what more do you want?
And as for you and me, we're through too, forever. I'll get even
with you if it's the last thing I ever do in my life. You think that
just because you're a great big lummox you can bulldoze me. Well,
let me tell you something. When I'm finished with you, you'll rue
the day you ever accused me of being a thief."

It was now evident to Rex Brantford that Gary had stolen
the money. Looking Gary straight in the eye, coldly and accusingly,
he said, "Gary, why did you steal that money? Why did you take
it? Did you really need it? If you had needed it for food or
clothing, I'm sure that people would have gladly given money to
you. Tell me why you took it."

For a moment, Gary was stunned. He fell back into the seat
and wilted.

"Reverend Brantford, I had a chance to take an airplane ride
to Harrisburg the other day. I'd never been in an airplane before
in my life. The pilot said he'd take me if I'd pay for the gas, so
I borrowed the money. I'm planning to pay it all back. Really,
I didn't steal it; I just borrowed it."

"But Gary, you had no right to borrow church funds which
you held in sacred trust, and it wasn't at all necessary for you to
take an airplane trip to Harrisburg, now was it? Incidentally,
just how and when do you plan to pay this money back?"

Gary shook his head and said, "I don't know."

Walking over to the boy, Rex put his hand on Gary's shoulder.
"Gary, we'll not tell a soul about this. I wouldn't think of turning
you over to the police, and I don't want the people in the church
to know about it either. God can forgive you, I know, and He
will if you'll ask Him, but the money must be replaced. I promised
the superintendent that this matter would be straightened out

by noon tomorrow, so do you think you could borrow fifty dollars and pay it back to the Sunday school treasury by tomorrow noon? Is there anyone who would loan it to you? Your parents, for instance?"

Gary shook his head. "Naw, I don't dare tell my ma. She'd beat me up."

Rex thought, *Gary must be taught a lesson. He must accept the responsibility of paying back the money he has stolen, otherwise he will repeat his error.*

"Gary, I expect you to get that money, legitimately, and to return it to me by tomorrow noon, but whatever you do, get the money in an honest Christian way. If you find that you aren't able to raise that amount by tomorrow noon, I want you to report back to me, in which case I'll see what I can do to help you. Now, before you leave, let's pray about this matter together, Gary."

They bowed their heads and Rex prayed, "Lord, please forgive Gary, and help him to repay the money he has stolen."

After he had finished his prayer, he suggested, "Gary, won't you pray now, asking the Lord to forgive you, and to assist you to rectify the wrong you've done?"

Gary shook his head negatively and slowly walked away with head bowed.

CHAPTER 3

REX BRANTFORD AROSE EARLY TUESDAY MORNING, made his sick calls and hastened to the church, so he would be there when Gary arrived.

When Gary did not show up by noon, he knelt beside his desk and prayed for him.

At one o'clock, Gary still had not arrived, so Rex telephoned Blanche and asked, "Have there been any telephone calls?"

"No," Blanche replied.

"Gary Streetland didn't phone?"

"No, why?"

"Oh, nothing, I just wanted to make sure. He was to meet me here at the office, but he never showed up."

"When will you be home for lunch, Rex? The food's cold now, so I'll have to warm it up again."

"I don't know. Better not wait lunch for me, because I have something very important to do which will take a little while."

Before leaving, Rex looked up and down the highway in both directions to make sure Gary was not on his way to the office.

It was thirty minutes later when he entered the bank in Port Allegheny. He introduced himself to the president of the bank, "I'm the new pastor of the Radford Community Church, Rex Brantford."

"Delighted to meet you," replied the president of the bank. "What can I do for you?"

"I expect to be opening an account with you shortly, but at present, my immediate need is a loan of fifty dollars."

"Well, Reverend Brantford, this is the first time I've met you, and it takes a little while to put a loan through. You understand our banking procedures, I'm sure."

"Yes, I understand your policies, but this situation is different. I want to save the reputation of a young lad."

"Whom, may I ask?"

"I would rather keep that confidential if you don't mind, but I must have the fifty dollars immediately if his reputation is to be saved."

"Do you have any securities for collateral on such a loan?"

"I have insurance, but after all, I'm a preacher, you know, and though I don't make much, my reputation and character should be good security."

"Not in a bank, Reverend Brantford. We must have real security. Do you have the policy with you?"

"Yes sir. Here it is."

The bank president examined the policy, then said, "All right, we'll give you the loan. On what basis can you make payments on this loan, Rev. Brantford?"

"It will mean plenty of squeezing to do it, but I'll repay the note within five weeks, ten dollars a week."

"That'll be just fine. Now, if you'll just be seated, I'll make out the necessary papers so you may sign them. Do you wish to open a checking account with us at this time, also?"

"Yes, I might as well, if you please."

Within five minutes, the bank president returned with the papers and said, "Just sign here, please."

As soon as Rex had affixed his signature to the papers, the president asked, "Would you like to place the fifty in your account? Then you can draw on it at leisure."

"Yes, please, and if you don't mind, I'll make out a check for fifty dollars and take the cash with me. I don't want anyone to know I borrowed this money, other than my wife."

Rex left the bank with fifty dollars and went directly to the office of Mr. Leighton in the nearby village.

"Good morning, Pastor!" Mr. Leighton greeted. "How did you make out with Gary?"

Without committing himself, Rex handed the fifty dollar bill to Mr. Leighton. "This should balance the Sunday school account, Mr. Leighton."

"Well, well. I wouldn't have believed it. Frankly, I didn't think Gary would ever pay back the money, because his mother has always protected him and spoiled him to such an extent the boy thinks he can get away with almost anything. He's been in one scrape after another, and this is the first time he has ever squared his accounts."

"Gary resigned as Sunday school treasurer, Mr. Leighton, but I'm sure that if we show him Christian love, he'll soon forget his grudge and get back into the harness again. I'm sure you will agree, we should do everything to encourage young people."

"Of course," Leighton agreed. "However, I must admit I'm glad he resigned as treasurer, because I simply don't trust him and he's better out."

As Rex left the office and drove home, he dreaded the prospect of telling Blanche what he had done. *I can just hear her scolding me in her loving way*, he thought. *She'll say, "Rex, you're always an easy mark. You shouldn't let people take advantage of you the way you do. Won't you ever learn that the more you do for people the less they seem to appreciate it, and they are the first ones to betray you?"*

But Blanche is a good girl, she'll see it my way after she has time to think. And I am right, for the Word says, "If thine enemy hunger, feed him; if he thirst, give him to drink: For in so doing thou shalt heap coals of fire on his head. Be not overcome with evil, but overcome evil with good." Isn't that what I preached last Sunday?

As he entered the parsonage, Blanche was at the door to meet him. He put his arms around her and kissed her. At the same time he looked at the threadbare rug and plain, outdated furniture, and a feeling of guilt crept over him. Blanche had so wanted to buy new furniture, but they just couldn't afford it. Nevertheless, he had borrowed fifty dollars and spent it to cover up the crime of a boy who had squandered that amount on a pleasure trip.

Before he had a chance to explain to Blanche, the phone rang. She left his embrace and went to the phone.

"It's for you," she said. "I'll warm up your lunch while you answer it."

"Hello. Rex Brantford speaking."

On the other end of the line a terrible explosion occurred. Rex could hear a woman screaming and crying at the top of her voice. "What do you mean by accusing my boy of being a common thief? My dear Gary."

"But . . . but . . . Mrs. Streetland, just a minute. Please, Mrs. Streetland, let me explain. Mrs. Streetland, won't you let me say just one word?"

On and on the tirade continued. It is dubious that Mrs. Streetland really needed a telephone, the way she was screaming. Rex was convinced that both he and all of the neighbors between the parsonage and the Streetland home could have easily heard her vindictive comments without the assistance of the telephone.

After seemingly endless minutes of this tongue-lashing, Blanche, who could hear the screaming, walked over to the phone and deliberately tried to break the connection, but Rex hindered her from doing so.

"You don't have to listen to those insults," Blanche insisted.

Though Rex's face was pale, he put his hand over the mouthpiece of the phone and smilingly replied, "The old top will finally run down, Blanche, so if I hang on long enough, I may be able to explain things to her."

Blanche herself was beginning to wonder just what had happened. She hadn't heard as yet.

Rex never did have an opportunity to make an explanation. He continued trying, but at last, with one scream of exhaustion, Maggie Streetland shouted, "I'll fix you! I'll fix you and good! I'll get even with you! If you only knew what was good for you, you'd pack up and get out of here right now! If you don't, you'll wish you had!"

Rex gazed at the suddenly silent phone for a few moments, dumbfounded, then he placed the receiver in the cradle.

Now he *was* convinced his wife wouldn't understand, nor would she approve the fifty-dollar loan he had made in order to protect Gary.

"What under the sun has happened?" Blanche asked with tears in her eyes.

Rex related the entire story from beginning to end. When he began to tell what Mrs. Streetland had said over the phone, Blanche commented philosophically, "That part won't be necessary, for I heard it as well as you did. I just wonder what that vindictive, vicious woman will do next? I tell you, Rex, she is dangerous, for she's practically out of her mind. She might set fire to our house or to the church!"

"Oh no, she would never do anything like that," Rex replied. "At least, I hope not." He stroked his chin thoughtfully and said, "You may be sure that she'll do something, though. Whatever she does, it will be devilish and subtle."

Rex sat with his head in his hands, pondering. Finally, he looked up and confessed, "Honey, we might as well pack up and leave here, the sooner the better."

Blanche ran her fingers through his hair. "Now Rex, you know you couldn't leave here if you would, for it would ruin your ministry and reputation all over the country. Furthermore, even if we didn't have to stay, you're too much of a man to run away from a Jezebel and allow her to have her way and ruin God's church. After all, God sent us here to minister to a needy people whom we already love, so we aren't leaving until we have won the victory through our Lord Jesus Christ. Our cause is just, our mission is noble, and our weapon is love; therefore, we cannot be defeated, for love is more powerful than hate, and God is on our side. We're sticking it out no matter what happens, and you know it."

Rex arose, put his arms around Blanche, and kissed her. "You're a dear, do you know that? I've got the best minister's wife in the world, and I'm proud of you. Of course we're going to stick it out, no matter what happens; it's only that . . . well, sometimes it's a little hard to walk by faith instead of by sight, for it's human to look for some cracks in the walls of Jericho when you are walking around them."

But that night Rex couldn't sleep, the burden of the situation rested so heavily upon his heart; nor could Blanche sleep. They tossed restlessly, until Blanche finally said, "Rex, can't you sleep, either?"

"No, I can't," he confessed. "It's not that I'm worried about the future or the final outcome of the affair with Gary and his mother; I'm deeply concerned about their spiritual welfare and particularly the boy's future. I'm afraid his life will be ruined if

I fail to reach him for Christ, and his mother isn't helping the situation any, either."

"I'll fix some hot chocolate," Blanche said, "then maybe we'll be able to sleep."

"I might as well get up, too," Rex said. "Can't sleep anyway. Let's go to the kitchen and have a word of prayer together, Blanche. What do you say?"

"Let's," was her reply.

CHAPTER 4

CHARLENE MAY HAVE LOOKED MUCH LIKE HER mother, but as far as her interests in life were concerned, she was more like her father. Though just slightly taller than her mother, she had the same lithe, graceful figure. She was like a floating sunbeam, vivacious and full of life.

The parsonage was situated just below the highway that wound its way along the side of the mountain. Not more than a hundred yards from the house at the bottom of the valley was the narrow, dashing, gurgling creek that laughed ceaselessly. The nearest house to the parsonage was that of the Hollands who lived about a half mile down the road. Most of the houses were scattered far apart along the valley. About three miles up the creek was a little village with a general store and eight or ten houses that had been built near the railroad station.

It was one of those bright, sunshiny, late June mornings when Charlene put on her father's black and white checkered wool hunting shirt, blue jeans, and boots. Throwing a creel over her shoulder, she took down the bamboo fly-casting rod. As she cautiously worked her way down the stream, carefully fishing each rapid and patiently casting ahead of the trout holes, she soon discovered that the trout were rising to just one fly — a green, female Drake with yellow eggs.

It was good to be alone with nature in the great out-of-doors which Charlene loved. On the side of the steep mountain which arose almost perpendicularly behind their house, she noticed deer grazing on what appeared to be bare ground. Then she heard the low drumming of a grouse, a sound seldom heard in the woods. She stood still, watching the grouse, and suddenly, to her amazement, he flew toward her, and setting his wings, he glided into a hemlock tree which grew near the edge of the creek. Moving stealthily downstream, she saw a large grayish animal, fascinated with his own occupation near the creek's edge. She watched him for a long time before he sniffed the air and fled into the forest. *What was that?* she wondered. Then, she remembered seeing a picture of a badger and thought that was likely what it was.

Now the stream widened, and the water became choppy as it moved swiftly over the gravel and rocks, but she soon discovered that the trout had retreated from the rapids to the deep, mysterious holes which formed at the bends of the creek, for the sun had now risen high on the horizon.

She cautiously worked her way along the shore, moving like a shadow, until she came to the lower edge of a hole where a tree had fallen, burying its limbs in the murky, mysterious depths. The waters swirled into eddies as they moved through the hole, gurgling out of existence on the lower side. *This is a perfect spot for a big rainbow to hide and feed on the food which is sucked to the bottom of the pool,* she thought.

After carefully surveying the situation so she would not blunder and spoil her chances of making a catch, she noted that there was a sand bar near shore which would be ideal for beaching a fish. Stepping slowly into the water, she began whipping her line, then dropped the fly so it fell at the bottom of the rapids. Skillfully, for she had learned much from her father in the last few weeks, she led the fly through the water to the mouth of the hole, taking care that there was no line drag which would cause the fly to move unrealistically and thus warn the trout away. She was tense with excitement. There was a quick, silvery flash in the pool, and her muscles reacted instantly, tightening the line by jerking the pole to one side. The pole bent over and the water began to boil!

Carefully she held the pole level and high above the water, following the fish's every move in order to keep an upward tension upon him. Once he tried to wrap the line around a large boulder, but she followed his circular path and hindered him. After being played for about ten minutes, suddenly the fish rushed for the depths of the hole where he would undoubtedly entangle the line about the tree top, break it, and make his getaway, but Charlene was too quick for him. Using his own momentum gained by speed, she guided him to the sand bar without attempting to lift him from the water.

It was then she saw he was poorly hooked, only in the cheek, so she reached down and held him with her two hands. He was slippery and as strong as steel, but before he could wriggle from her grasp, she was on shore and threw him to the bank. At last she had him in her creel, and he was so large his tail hung out through the hole in the lid. She was so excited she cried aloud as if someone were with her to share her great victory.

It was not until the battle was won that she heard the whine of a cat in the huge poplar tree overhead. She became so frightened, she hurried back to the creek. Now she looked up to locate him. An unexpected voice behind her said, "You throw a pretty line! Congratulations! I saw you catch him . . . I've tried many times but wasn't a good-enough fisherman to outwit him."

Charlene was so startled and frightened, she became faint. Quickly she whirled around and saw a young man about her age, standing among the rhododendrums. When she saw his rugged, honest face, her fears left her. She couldn't help but admire his handsome features, his warm smile, and his brown, curly hair. He was just as she would want him to be.

Tossing her head to one side with her golden hair falling across her shoulders, she gave a friendly smile and invited him to draw nearer.

"Hi ya, and who are you?" she asked.

"I'm Dick Holland. I live just below you in the house down the valley."

"Oh! I'm glad to meet you. My name's Charlene Brantford; I'm the preacher's daughter."

"Yes, I know; I've been wanting to get acquainted with you. By the way, what fly are you using? You seem to be having pretty good results with it, aren't you?"

"Yes, they're hitting good this morning on a green, female Drake with yellow eggs. Last week they were taking the Royal Coachman, and the week before, father caught a two-pounder on a Silver King."

"You really know your flies, don't you? I didn't think a girl would ever take fishing so seriously, but you seem to know your way around. Been fishing long?"

"No, just since we moved here, but I go fishing every day. It took me two weeks to catch my first fish; since then, I've sort of caught on to the trick of it. Daddy taught me how to fish; he's an old timer. I'm not so much interested in catching fish as in the trees, the birds, the wild flowers and nature in general."

"Yeah. By the way, when you get back of our house, you'll find a fresh spring feeding into the creek, and there's lots of fresh, crisp watercress growing. Help yourself to it, anytime. There's mint there, too."

"Oh, thanks. I will."

"Do you folks like mountain tea? There's lots of it growing up on the mountainside."

"I wouldn't know it if I saw it. What's it look like?"

"It belongs to the mint family. I'll get you some; if you've never drunk mountain tea, you've missed the most refreshing drink nature offers. Did you ever eat poke?"

"What's poke?"

"I can see you're from the city! I'll have to show you around the woods. Poke makes wonderful greens, a lot better than spinach, and it's for free, too."

"What are those little red berries on the mountain top? I wondered if they were poison or eatable?"

"Those? Teaberries. Did you ever chew teaberry gum? Same flavor. The grouse feed on them. I don't know whether you hunt or not, but if you do, you will generally find the grouse feeding near the top of the mountain on those teaberries. Last winter, while on stand, deer hunting, I filled my cap with teaberries while waiting for the drive to start, and a big buck must have heard the hunters coming, for he jumped right over a log where I was picking berries. There I was, caught unprepared without my gun, with a cap full of teaberries, so I dropped the berries, grabbed my gun and took a quick shot at the fleeing deer just as it disappeared out of sight. Did I get the raspberries!"

"Daddy's promised to buy me a twenty-gauge shotgun this fall, that is, if he can afford it, and if he does, I'm going to try to shoot some grouse."

"They sure are fast," Dick said, "so don't feel bad if you can't hit 'em. There aren't many hunters ever hit one, but it's fun trying. I'd like to take you and your father hunting, so I can show you where they are, if you'll let me, come hunting season."

Charlene's face brightened. "Would you? I'd be delighted."

"It's a date, then?"

"It's a date. Incidentally, why don't you come to Christian Endeavor at the church this Sunday night? There's lots of kids there you know, and I'm sure you'd like it. I wish you would."

"If you'll be there, I'll come."

"Good! I'll be looking for you. We meet six thirty to seven thirty, closing when the evening service begins."

Dick hesitated, but finally worked up enough courage to ask, "Would it be all right if I'd pick you up and take you?"

Charlene's face turned a warm red. She swallowed and answered, "I'd be delighted."

"I'll be at your house, then, about six-fifteen. I better be going now; I'm supposed to be chopping wood for the kitchen stove, and if I don't show up soon, Mom'll be all upset. It's been nice talking with you. Don't forget to help yourself to some watercress and mint when you get back of our house."

"Thanks. I'll be seeing you Sunday."

Dick reached for a small tree to lift himself as he climbed over a huge boulder and started up the steep mountain, then he hesitated and looked back. Charlene was already whipping her line over a gurgling hole in the creek when he called to her again.

"Charlene!" he almost swallowed as he called her first name. It sounded too familiar having just met her.

Charlene looked up quizzically and waited for him.

"Charlene, I wouldn't fish too far down the stream if I were you."

"Why not?"

"Well, I don't like to say this but our neighbors down below, the Streetlands, get pretty mean if anyone crosses over their property. Jake, the old man, is drunk half of the time and he might even come out and threaten to shoot you. You never know what that old codger is going to do. He's about the meanest man around here."

"Oh!" exclaimed Charlene. "Thanks for telling me. I'll just work down far enough to get some of that watercress and mint, and then I'll fish back to our house."

"Let me go down with you and help you pick the watercress and mint."

"Sure, come on."

It was late afternoon when Charlene returned home with a half dozen nice trout. As she handed them to her mother, she had a faraway, dreamy look.

"Charlene," her mother said.

"Charlene! Where are you? Aren't you listening?"

"Oh, excuse me. Yes, Mother, what is it?"

"You caught the fish, now how about cleaning them?"

"Oh, I'm so tired, Mother. Would you do it for me?"

"No, ma'am. I've just made a new rule in this house that whoever gets fish or game must clean their own catch, so it's up to you to get them ready to fry for supper. Here's a knife, and you can put some newspaper on the drainboard of the sink and get to work."

"Oh, my, I'm so tired, but . . . well, I might as well get it over with."

Charlene stuck up her nose and touched the fish lightly, then biting her lip and frowning intently, she began her task by cutting off the head of the smallest fish. Her next move was to cut the dorsal fin from the fish, but in the process the knife slipped and she cut her thumb.

"Ow!" she screamed.

"Now what have you done?" her mother scolded.

"Oh, Mother, look! It's bleeding!"

"Here. Let me have that knife; I might as well do it myself. You go and get a band-aid and bandage up that finger and then hurry back and help me get the supper on the stove. You can do that much anyway."

Mother had almost finished cleaning the fish when Charlene returned.

"Say, Mother, guess what?"

"What?"

"I met Dick Holland this morning."

"The neighbor boy who lives just below us?"

"That's right. And is he handsome!"

"You sound as if you might like him."

"Yes, I do, Mother. He's really handsome, and the nicest fellow I think I ever met. I invited him to attend our Christian Endeavor Sunday night, and he promised he would come. Better yet, he asked me if he could take me with him."

"Sounds like you asked for a date." Blanche's eyes were laughing with amusement.

"Mother! You know better than that; I'm a lady."

"Are you sure he didn't catch these fish?"

"Of course not. Mother, Daddy will be thrilled when he hears I caught that big one. Dick said he had been trying to catch him for a long time, but he always got away from him, so he thinks I'm some fisherman."

"How did he know you caught it? Did you show it to him?"

"No. He was standing watching all the time I caught him, and

I didn't even know he was there until after I had the fish on shore. He almost got away from me, too. Wasn't hooked very good, only in the cheek. When Dick spoke to me I jumped almost a foot high, I guess, I was so surprised. He just suddenly came from nowhere, out of thin air, just like in story books. Oh, Mother, he's wonderful!"

Blanche and Charlene were just putting supper on the table when Rex came in. He sniffed the air and said, "Smells like you had a good day, Charlene. Tell me about it."

"I got the limit! And I caught a great big one, as big or bigger than the one you caught the other day."

"That's not all she caught," Blanche said.

"No?" Rex asked quizzically.

"I should say not; she caught herself a new beau, too."

Rex's eyes twinkled and he smiled.

Charlene put on an air of disgust though she was inwardly pleased, and she scolded, "Mother! You don't have to tell everything you know."

"That's good news," Rex said, grinning broadly. "I was beginning to fear we had an old maid on our hands for the rest of our lives."

"Daddy! That's no joke. Dick's really a nice boy."

"Oh, I'm sure of that. Well, let's get to something more important; I'm hungry," he said as he sat down at the table.

After they had said the blessing, Charlene looked off into space and said dreamily, "Dick is really wonderful."

CHAPTER 5

"WHAT'S THAT?" REX ASKED IN A STARTLED TONE when Dick Holland drove up to the parsonage in a car with four wheels, plenty of slogans painted on the side, no top and no fenders.

"Daddy! It's not that bad. After all, a young man can't afford a Cadillac."

Rex grinned. "It's all right, dear. After all, it isn't so far to the church but what you can walk if the garbage truck breaks down."

Charlene stamped her foot with implied anger, but actually with delight. "Oh, you!"

Just then Dick laid on the horn with all his weight, at least it sounded like it. All horns on the car, including those he had just added the last week, resounded with enthusiasm. Charlene went running out the front door and jumped in. She waved as the rattle-trap roared away.

Rex slapped his knee and laughed uproariously. "You'd think he would at least come to the door and play the Romeo on his first date," he said.

"You're still living in the Victorian age," Blanche said. "Don't criticize the boy. After all, he's probably scared of so auspicious a character as the right Reverend Mister Rex Brantford, the famous divine of the most outstanding pulpit in the whole valley, in fact the only one."

"I smell sarcasm in that statement," Rex said, smiling.

"I think he's a nice boy," Blanche said seriously.

"So do I," Rex agreed. "Oh, to be young again. Do you remember when I called on you and took you out on your first date? I wore the latest belted-coat suit with balloon trousers and you wore a mixing bowl upside down on your head."

"Yes. Only I had to walk to church with you. At least, the modern generation has advanced to a car just one jump ahead of the junk heap, and that's something."

"Now don't criticize my transportation in those days, Blanche; walking is good for the health, and besides, it costs less than gasoline. Young people would be better off if they didn't have it so easy these days." Rex glanced at his watch. "We'd better leave, or we'll be late for church, don't you think?"

"I'm ready whenever you are," Blanche retorted.

They hadn't gone more than half way to the church when they saw Dick and Charlene stranded alongside the road, so Rex pulled up beside them. "What's the matter?"

"Out of gas," Dick said with embarrassment. "Could you give us a lift, Reverend Brantford?" he asked.

"Sure, jump in."

"Daddy, you never met Dick, did you?" Charlene said as she climbed into the car. "And this is my mother, too, Dick."

"Glad to meet you," Dick said with embarrassment.

"Would you like to stop at a filling station so you can get some gas?" Rex asked.

"No, thanks; we're apt to be late if we bother to get gas now. Besides, I . . . well, I'll come get the car tomorrow morning."

Rex guessed the boy's predicament and said no more. *Probably doesn't have any money,* he thought.

When they arrived at the church, some of the young people were standing outside, waiting until the last minute before going inside.

"Hi, Dick," Charles Larson called. "What got you out to church? I never thought even Charlene could get you here."

"Chuck!" Charlene said with disgust. "You certainly aren't very kind."

"If they don't want me here, maybe I better not go in," Dick said to Charlene. "After all, I don't belong here."

"You belong here as much as anyone else," Charlene said. "Don't pay any attention to Chuck; he's just one person, and I must say he isn't very courteous. He ought to be ashamed of himself."

Dick hesitated, so Charlene took his hand and started inside the church. "Come on. You'll have a good time."

Charlene was one of five speakers that evening, so when she arose, she prayed silently, "Dear Lord, please help me to say something that will bring Dick to Christ. He's such a nice fellow, but he needs the Lord; that's all that's lacking."

She watched him all the time she was speaking. He listened to her intently, as she purposely fished for his soul with greater skill than she had fished for trout, and he seemed to sense it. He proved to be more wily than the fish, however, and escaped being hooked.

I wish I could throw the net of the Gospel and catch souls as good as I can fish, Charlene thought.

Dick and Charlene sat together in church that evening, of course, and she prayed for him throughout the service, but when the invitation was given, she noticed he became extremely fidgety and struggled to escape making a decision. He appeared almost relieved when the invitation ended and the benediction was offered. He talked little while the Brantfords drove him home, and when they reached his house, Charlene invited, "Wouldn't you like to go on home with us for a little while?"

"I think I'd better not," he replied. "Thanks, though."

Charlene was silent until they arrived home.

"What's the matter, Charlene?" Mother asked. "You seem bothered about something. What is it?"

"Mother, I tried so hard to win Dick to Christ tonight, but somehow I failed. He seems farther away from a decision than before."

"But darling, you can't expect to win him to Christ the very first night! Soul winning doesn't come that easy. It takes time and patience."

"I don't see why. I caught that fish the first try; why can't I catch souls as easy?"

"Didn't Dick tell you he had been trying to catch that fish for many months and he couldn't? You just happened along at the right time when conditions were just right. You mustn't get discouraged; you will win Dick yet."

"I hope so," Charlene said and wiped tears from her eyes.

"Don't take it so hard, Sweetheart," Rex said as he put his arm about her and kissed her. "Let's pray about it. What do you say?"

Charlene looked up through her tears and nodded.

After prayer she said, "Now I feel better. I believe God will save him when it is His time, but I just hope nothing happens to interfere with his salvation."

"Come on now, let's all have a cup of chocolate before we go to bed," Blanche said.

CHAPTER 6

SATURDAY, TWO WEEKS LATER, BLANCHE AND REX were eating an early breakfast, and Charlene was still sleeping. Blanche said, "I'm worried about Charlene."

"What seems to be the trouble?" he asked.

"Haven't you noticed how morose and blue she seems to be? For the past two weeks she hasn't eaten hardly anything, and she doesn't go anywhere or do anything. I wonder what's troubling her?"

"You're her mother; why don't you talk to her and find out?" Rex suggested.

"I think I will. She always confides everything in me, but this time she's as silent as a sphinx."

"Well," Rex said as he pushed himself away from the table, "I guess I'd better get going; I've much to do this morning. Good-by, now. I'll be home for lunch this noon." He kissed her and was gone. He always left in a hurry.

Blanche was putting the last dishes in the cupboard when Charlene came down stairs. "Good morning, Charlene," she said. "How about some bacon and eggs for breakfast?"

"I don't think so, Mother. I don't feel like eating. I'll just drink some orange juice and a cup of coffee, and maybe a piece of toast."

"Charlene, dear, tell me what's wrong. Something's bothering you. What is it?"

"Nothing."

"Yes, it is something. Is it Dick?"

Charlene was silent, then she burst into tears. "He hasn't come near me since Sunday night. I guess he doesn't like me. Otherwise, he would at least telephone, don't you think?"

"There may be nothing wrong. I imagine he's just a little timid and afraid to come around, but if you'll give him time, you'll see him again soon."

"I'm afraid I drove him away, trying to win him for Christ. I shouldn't have said as much as I did. Now I've ruined it all."

"If he doesn't want Christ, then you don't want him, Charlene. However, I wouldn't be so quick to jump to conclusions. Just wait and see."

"That's easy to say," Charlene replied.

She picked at her food and finally left the table without eating much.

"Charlene," her mother called. "Why don't you go trout fishing? It'll help you to forget your troubles, and who knows, you might just happen to see Dick."

"Oh, Mother, I'm not chasing after him. That would be the wrong thing."

"Of course not. You wouldn't be chasing after him, only fishing. You love to fish, so why don't you try fishing that same hole where you caught the big one? Another, even bigger fish, might be lurking there."

Charlene spoke slowly, "I think I will."

Blanche watched her as she walked back of the house to the creek. *She's so sweet,* she thought. *I hate to see her troubled.*

Charlene didn't waste much time fishing the stream directly back of the house, but hurried to the big hole just below the Holland place. She caught two small fish in the hole, then moved on downstream. She kept watching out of the corner of her eye to see if Dick were around, though she was making every effort to convince herself that she wasn't really looking for him.

She went farther downstream than ever before, and discovered another creek emptying into the stream, whereupon the water became more violent and deeper, causing the current to increase considerably. Beaver had built a dam a few hundred feet below, creating a pond, but there was a deep hole just before the creek widened. The current became extremely swift, so she cautiously stepped into the current to a position where she could cast her fly above the hole. The rocks were slippery and without warning, her foot slipped and she fell into the swift, cold, moving water which swept her into the deep hole. Her boots filled with water and became as heavy as lead. She screamed as she fell, but once in the water, she was helpless, and though she fought to save herself, it was in vain, until, finally, she lost consciousness.

The first she knew, after that, was the sound of Dick's voice, which seemed far off. He was administering first aid and calling, "Charlene, Charlene, do you hear me?"

"Where am I?" she asked as she opened her eyes. "What happened? Where am I?"

"You almost drowned, Charlene. I heard your cry, but by the time I got here, you were under the water and had lost consciousness. I didn't think you would ever come out of it; I had about given up hope until I breathed air into your lungs. Are you all right, now?"

"I guess so. I feel so weak and cold." She shivered and her teeth chattered. Her lips and fingernails were purple.

"You'd better take it easy for a few minutes. As soon as you're able to walk, we'll go up to my house, and I'll drive you home. I don't think you should try to walk it."

Charlene lay breathing heavily, and for some inexplainable reason she couldn't help but cry. After she had regained her self-control, she said, "I'm sorry. I guess it's a woman's privilege to cry, isn't it? I couldn't help myself."

"Cry if you want to," Dick said. "All I care is that you're well enough to cry. For a minute, I thought you were a goner, for sure. Feeling better now?"

"Yes, I think I can make it to the house now. Let me take off these boots first, so I can pour the water out." Just look at me! I look like a drowned rat."

Dick helped her to get up. Just then they heard a gruff, violent voice shouting, "Get off my property before I have you arrested!" The man emphasized his command with epithets of cursing. Charlene looked up and in dismay saw a man about fifty years of age, mousy-looking, with bushy eyebrows and a big chin. His nose hooked down in an effort to meet his protruding chin, and his moustache swirled downward, evidently in keeping with his nasty temper.

"Mr. Streetland," Dick answered, "this is the minister's daughter, if you please, and you'd do well to watch your language."

"All the more reason she should stay off my property. If she's a Christian, she should know better than to trespass and break the law. Now get your carcasses off my property before I have you both arrested. Ought to, anyhow."

"Mr. Streetland, Charlene almost drowned down at the big hole, and 'she is in no condition to hurry, so I'm afraid you'll just have to be a little patient, whether you like it or not."

"Serves her right for getting on my property. Maybe she'll have enough sense to stay away from here in the future. That trout hole is reserved strictly for Gary. Now get off my property! I'm telling you for the last time, get off!" he bellowed.

"Don't pay any attention to him," Dick said. "Here, let me help you. If he gets too rambunctious, I'll settle him down."

"Please don't fight," Charlene pled. "I'm at fault, for I shouldn't have been on his property in the first place. Really, I didn't mean to; I didn't know I was as far downstream as his place."

"You know, Charlene, that's one thing I just can't understand. There's that Mrs. Streetland, who professes to be such a good Christian, and her husband acts meaner than Satan. It just doesn't make sense."

"Does he profess to be a Christian, Dick?"

"I guess not, but you can't blame him, not with the wife he has. She'd drive any man crazy. She even gets on my nerves, living so close to us."

"Dick, the trouble with you is, you have your eyes on people instead of on Christ. Is there anything wrong with Jesus?"

"No. But Christians claim that they are changed when Christ enters their heart and they are saved. Yet I'm more of a gentleman than the Streetlands if I do say so myself. Still I make no claim to be a Christian."

"Dick, each one of us must stand before God on our own record, and I can't judge the Streetlands. It's not for me to know whether they are saved or not; I hope they are, but the important thing is, are you saved?"

"No, I'm not."

"I wish you were," Charlene said.

Dick was startled. "What difference does it make?"

"Well, just suppose I had drowned . . . I almost did . . . where would I be right now, in that case?"

"You? In heaven, there's no doubt about that. You're a good girl. Too good for me."

"No, I'm not too good for you. There's none good, no not one, but I would be in heaven had I drowned, not because of my goodness, but because Jesus' death on the cross for my sins saved me. And Dick, Jesus will save you if you'll but ask Him. Why don't you?"

"Not now."

"Why not?"

"Don't push me, Charlene. When I'm good and ready, I'll become a Christian, but first, I intend to have a good time."

"Now is God's time; you may not have a chance later. How easy it is to suddenly leave this world without warning. Little did I know, when I started out this morning, I would be so close to eternity, and if it weren't for you, I would be dead right now. Thanks, Dick, for saving my life."

"Don't thank me. I'm just glad I happened along at the right time and heard you scream, otherwise I never would have known you needed help, and you would be dead now."

In the distance, they could still faintly hear Mr. Streetland swearing and shouting at them.

"That old codger!" Dick said with irritation. "If he doesn't shut up, I'm going back there and give him the walloping he deserves. Must be out of his head."

"Oh, forget him, Dick. You know what?"

"What?"

"You saved my life; I'd like to save yours."

"How come?"

"I'd like to give you eternal life."

Dick's face grew red. He didn't answer. Charlene decided it was time to drop the subject, so she did.

Dick drove her home, and when they arrived, he helped her from the car and walked with her to the front door.

Blanche met them at the door and asked in dismay, "What happened? You look so pale, Charlene, and you're soaking wet!"

"She almost drowned," Dick said.

"Dick saved my life, Mother."

"Oh, Charlene! My precious girl! Dick, won't you come in? I'm so thankful to you for saving her."

"I better be going now," Dick said. "She'll be all right, Mrs. Brantford; I wouldn't worry about her. Good-by, Charlene."

"Good-by, Dick, and thanks again."

CHAPTER 7

"BLANCHE, DO YOU THINK WE COULD AFFORD TO BUY the shotgun I promised Charlene?" Rex asked casually on a late August Saturday morning at the breakfast table.

Blanche refilled his cup of coffee before answering, "I don't see how we can afford it; not after paying that loan you made to square Gary's account. I just can't understand it. His mother comes out in a new outfit about once a month, and yet they'll let the preacher pay his debt and never say a word about it. If I were she, I'd be ashamed to show my face in church again. She's got nerve."

"But you aren't Maggie Streetland, therefore you'll never be able to comprehend the idiosyncrasies of so charming a lady. Anyway, that's not the point; I made a promise to Charlene, and I don't think she should suffer because of what Gary did."

"Yes, I agree," Blanche began to soften, "nevertheless we don't have the money, and I don't see how we can afford it."

"We could buy it on time, couldn't we?"

"Yes. But I don't like to buy things on time. It's against my principles."

"It's not a good policy, I'll admit," Rex said with a frown, "but I'm afraid it's the only way she'll ever get that shot-gun. I think they'll let me pay a dollar a week at the hardware store without paying any interest."

"In that case, let's get her the gun. She's so anxious to hunt with you and . . ." a smile broke over Blanche's face ". . . Dick promised to go with you and show you where the grouse are."

Rex went to the bottom of the stairs and called, "Charlene! You'd better get up and come down to breakfast. Do you hear me?"

There was no answer.

"Charlene! Wake up! I want to take you shopping."

"What for, Daddy?" Charlene answered.

"To buy that shotgun so you can go grouse hunting with Dick and me this November."

Charlene was wide awake and bouncing down the stairs immediately.

"Really, Daddy? Are you really going to buy it for me today?"

"You're the only boy I have, aren't you? If you had a brother, you'd be doomed to washing dishes like any other girl, so you're just fortunate. Yes, ma'am! We're getting it this very morning. Hurry and eat your breakfast, so we can go."

"What would you like?" Mother asked. "How about some scrapple and fried potatoes?"

"Uhmmm. Sounds good. And a cup of coffee."

Charlene was so excited, her eyes were wide and her face beamed as she plunged into eating breakfast, not picking at it as she usually did.

"Daddy, what kind of gun are you going to buy me?"

"I thought I'd buy you a .410 Winchester pump gun. They're nice and light and easy to handle. Just right for a girl. I'm afraid the .20 gauge might be a little too much for you."

"Whatever you say, Daddy. I don't know much about it." She gobbled down her last bit of food and ran upstairs, calling as she went, "I'll be ready in five minutes."

"Never saw her so excited," Rex said with a smile of satisfaction.

"She's surely changed since we moved to the mountains," Blanche mused. "A city girl would never think of owning a shotgun."

"Yes, it's good for her to roam the mountains; in fact, the youth of America would be much better off if they did more of that. God made the woods for dreaming, the fresh air to be breathed, but most people don't even know life as God planned it. I've been amazed at the wild flowers that girl has gathered while in the woods this summer. She's studied them until she can name almost every wild flower that grows."

"I'm ready, Daddy! Let's go!" Charlene called as she came bounding down the stairs. "Are you going with us, Mother?"

"No. I guess not. Buying guns is a little out of my line. You and Daddy can handle it all right without me."

"'By, Mom," Charlene said and kissed her hurriedly.

It took about thirty minutes to drive to the hardware store in Port Allegheny. They had a splendid stock of guns in preparation for the hunting season. Charlene soon held a .410 gauge shot-gun to her shoulder.

"I like this one," she said.

"If you like it, I'll buy it," Rex said.

Just then, Dick Holland walked into the store.

"Hello, Charlene," he said. "And you, too, Rev. Brantford."

"Oh, Dick, you came just in time," Charlene said. "Father's buying me a shot-gun. Look at this one. How do you like it?"

Dick took the gun and held it to his shoulder. "It's a honey," he said, "but it'll be hard to hit anything with it. It takes a good shot to hit anything with a .410; the twenty-gauge would be better."

The clerk spoke quickly, "That's true, but a .410 is quicker handling, and there's less kick to it. Just the thing for a girl."

"What do you think, Daddy?" Charlene asked dubiously.

Before Rex could answer, the clerk said, "You can now get three-inch shells for the .410 with an equal load to the twenty. I think this's the gun for you."

"It's a nice gun, all right," Dick agreed, "only it'll require a good shot to use it, and it'll be in my favor, because I'll be able to outshoot you." Dick grinned broadly.

"I'll take the .410," Charlene snapped. "I'll just show you men that a woman can shoot."

"Wrap it up," Rex said to the clerk, "and here's a five spot as a down payment. I'll finish paying it as agreed, a dollar a week. Oh, yes, better give us a couple of boxes of shells, the two and a half inch, so this girl can practice up. We don't want to make her look too bad when hunting season rolls around."

"You're really going hunting with me this fall, then?" Dick asked. His face brightened with enthusiasm.

"Correction! We're both going hunting with you, Dick," Rex said. "You're stuck with me, too."

"Oh, of course, that's what I intended all the time."

While the clerk was busy wrapping up the gun, Dick and Charlene chatted together. Rex excused himself, "Charlene, you wait here for the gun, and I'll go down the street and start buying the groceries for Mother. When you're ready, meet me at the grocery store."

"All right, Daddy." After Rex had left, Charlene said to Dick, "Why don't you ever come to Christian Endeavor? You've not been back since the first night. Didn't you like it?"

"Yes, only . . ."

"Only what? Did I do something or say something to offend you?"

"No, I should say not! I would love to be with you at C. E. every Sunday night, only . . . well, I don't like to say it."

"Please tell me. I've wondered if something were wrong, or if I did something I shouldn't have."

"I tell you, it's not you."

"Then what is it?"

Dick hesitated. "Oh, it's just that . . . it's what Chuck said."

"You mean that jibe he made when we drove up to the church?"

"No. It was what he said the next day He said, 'You've got your nerve trying to rush Charlene. You don't even belong to the church. Keep your hands off her, or else.'"

"Oh . . . Dick! Who does he think he is? I'm no chattel, and I'll go with whom I please, but there's one person I won't go with, and that's Chuck Larson. He's too short, and that's not all; he's too roughshod and dumb."

"It's not only Chuck; Gary seems to think he has a corner on you, too."

"Dick, you don't really think I would ever go with either of them, do you?"

"It's not that, either. It's that, well, I don't know how to say it, but I guess, well, they're trying to run a closed corporation at that church, and if that's the way they want it, I'm not coming around and break up their little private club."

"Listen, Dick, how many times must I tell you that Gary and Chuck aren't the whole church? It doesn't matter what they think or say, the church is for everyone and we want everyone to feel welcome. We want you there; I want you there, so please forget those two. Will you come this Sunday night?"

Dick hesitated. "All right, Charlene, I'll come."

"Good. I'll be looking for you."

"Here's your gun, Miss," the clerk interrupted. "Hope you like it. It's really a nice one."

"I just love it," Charlene answered, "and I'll show these fellows a thing or two."

"And here's the shells; don't forget them."

"Good-by, Dick. I'll see you Sunday night."

"Oh, Charlene, may I take you to the Christian Endeavor Sunday night?"

"I'd be delighted."

"Pick you up at a quarter after six then?"

"Uh-huh," Charlene replied and smiled contentedly as she pushed her way through the door.

As soon as Charlene reached home, she took the gun and started practicing. While helping her mother prepare supper that evening, she told her about the conversation with Dick. "Mother," she asked, "how can we ever win souls to Christ when people act the way Gary and Chuck do? You'd think they weren't at all interested in winning souls to Christ."

"Charlene, are you sure Gary and Chuck are saved? Maybe we should start by trying to win them to Christ. At least, if they are saved, they need to be taught the need of winning the lost. There are many Christians who have never caught the vision of witnessing to lost souls, and they have no burden whatsoever for them. They have never stopped to consider the terrible plight of the lost, for they have never given a thought to the awful future of those who die without Christ and go into a Christless grave and a Christless eternity."

"Mother, I do so want to win Dick to Christ, but it seems everything is against me."

"Just don't forget to win the others to Christ also," Mother reminded. "I tremble for Gary particularly. I doubt if he has ever been saved, and if something doesn't happen to straighten him out, soon, very soon, some tragedy will surely overtake him."

CHAPTER 8

THE LEAVES ON THE TREES IN THE ALLEGHENY Mountains had turned to a brilliant, glorious circus of color. In few places in the world do the leaves turn to as brilliant a red, as bright a yellow, or as rich a gold as they do in the Alleghenies in early October. The pine, spruce, and hemlock trees seem to huddle together in the midst of the dashing colors of fall as if they were trying to keep each other warm. The fresh cool breezes sigh through the pine needles foretelling the soon coming of winter. The black squirrel, native to this section, makes haste to strip the trees of their beechnuts in preparation for the bleak, wintry snows that would soon swirl about the mountainsides. It was the season of the year that invited hayrides, wiener roasts, and hard time parties.

At the Young People's Meeting at the little white church on a Sunday night in October, when an announcement was made of a coming hayride, Dick whispered to Charlene, "Do you think I could go on the hayride, too?"

"Why sure. It's for all the young people. We'd just love to have you go along."

"How about us going together?"

"There's nothing I'd like better, Dick."

The hayride started from the church promptly at six-thirty. More came than had been expected. Some of the young people who lived in the valley, though they never attended church, heard about the hayride and phoned Reverend Brantford to ask if they could go too.

It was a jolly crowd that drove down the road. Charlene and Dick were sitting together on the hay near the front of the wagon. Everyone seemed to be having a good time until Gary Streetland started shoving some of the girls off the wagon. When one of them sprained her ankle as she fell, Rex said, "Gary, that's enough of that roughhousing. You'd better stop it before someone gets hurt real bad."

Gary then looked around until he spied Charlene and Dick, whereupon he boldly tried to shove Dick aside and sit between them. "Move over, you drip," he said with sarcasm, "so a guy can sit down."

"You don't have to sit here," Dick said, glaring at him.

"Where'd you pick up the boy friend, Charlene?" Gary said, ignoring Dick. "Couldn't you come up with anyone better? Ha!"

"Gary, you're certainly rude," Charlene fumed with disgust. "Why can't you leave us alone?"

Using both hands, Gary grabbed Charlene and started to pull her off the wagon.

"Take your hands off her," Dick ordered.

"You try and make me," Gary threatened with a sneer on his face.

By that time, Charlene had wrenched herself away from Gary and said, "You aren't funny, Gary, you're rude. Now please, go away and leave us alone."

Dick's eyes burned with hate. He had almost reached the point of explosion, and Charlene knew it, so she arose, and balancing herself by holding onto Dick's shoulder, she moved to the other side of him.

"A fine one you are," Gary sneered. "As a preacher's daughter, you're a wash-out. Oh well, I don't intend to sit by this goof." Gary moved away.

When they reached the farm where they were to have devotions and a wiener roast, a huge bonfire was already spitting red embers into the black sky, and the air was fragrant with the aroma of hot coffee.

"Everyone off," Rex called. "There's enough hot dogs for all, and marshmallows, too. Help yourself."

"May I roast a hot dog for you?" Dick asked Charlene.

"Oh, thanks," Charlene answered.

As soon as Dick had put a wiener on the end of a fork and moved to the fire to roast it, Gary came to Charlene and whispered, "Hey, Charlene, let's leave here. We can have a better time elsewhere."

Charlene's face grew hot with anger. She almost slapped Gary in the face, but her better judgment took charge before her intuition had led her to do something she would have regretted afterward.

"Leave me alone, Gary," she said with disgust as she arose and moved closer to Dick and the fire.

"If that Dick Holland thinks he can horn in and take you away from me, I'll fix him in short order," Gary threatened.

"Whoever led you to believe that I belonged to you, Gary Streetland? I think I ought to have something to say about that," she retorted.

Gary's eyes were aflame with hate. He stepped back into the shadows, and Charlene thought he had left the party, for she didn't see him again.

After the wiener roast, Rex spoke to the group briefly, using Romans 12:1, 2 as his text to challenge them to dedicate their lives fully to Christ. Charlene watched Dick cautiously. He appeared to be under deep conviction, for moisture arose in his eyes, and he wiped it away with his sleeve.

At the conclusion of the message, Rex urged the young people to drop an evergreen on the fire as a symbol of their yieldedness to Christ. He said, "Will you put your all on the altar, and give up all self ambition for His sake? Let us give our lives to be burned out for Him."

As different ones began to move forward, Dick hesitated. He fidgeted with the evergreen he held in his hand as he battled within his own soul. He was at the point of decision.

Suddenly, out of the shadows of darkness a figure stole up behind Dick and, striking like a serpent, without warning, he locked his arm around his neck in a deadly grip. Dick staggered, choked and stumbled to the ground. When Charlene saw that it was Gary, she tried to break his tight grip on Dick's throat, but her efforts were in vain. She began to kick Gary's hands until, at last, he was compelled to release his death clutch.

Dick was on his feet in a moment and hit Gary a staggering blow in the pit of his stomach.

As soon as Gary could straighten up, he drew a yellow-handled, switchblade knife from his hip pocket and lunged for Dick. He slashed back and forth, trying to stab Dick, but his prey was too quick and nimble for him.

By this time, some of the other fellows had awakened to what was happening and fought to disarm Gary. Pinning his arms behind his back, they finally subdued him.

"So you call yourself a Christian?" Dick sneered at Gary. "If this is Christianity, I want none of it."

Dick walked away into the shadows and started to walk home, but Charlene ran after him, and overtaking him, she grasped his arm, drawing him back. "Please, Dick. Don't blame me for what Gary did."

Dick's face was solemn; anger still smoldered within his breast. Remaining silent, he returned with Charlene.

"I'm sorry," Rex said to Dick. "You musn't take it too seriously. Gary's always starting a fight: it's his nature, I guess."

Dick didn't answer.

Rex watched Gary carefully during the ride home, and took care to see to it that he didn't go near Dick and Charlene again.

When Dick and Charlene arrived home that night, she looked up into his face and said, "Please, Dick, don't allow what happened tonight to make you bitter. You will come back to C.E., won't you?"

"I don't think so. Charlene. I like you, but I can't see the kind of hypocritical Christianity they have down at that church. I want no more of it."

"But Dick, it's only Gary. Don't blame the rest of us."

"He's a part of the church, isn't he?"

He looked at Charlene, took her hands in his and said, "You're a wonderful girl, a beautiful girl; I think you're just great. I'll see you again, but I'm not going back to that church anymore."

Charlene was crying when she entered the front door.

"What's the matter, Charlene?"

"Mother, Dick was just about to accept Christ as his Saviour when Gary drove him away forever. I'll never win him to Christ now."

"Tell me, what happened?"

Charlene bolted up the stairs and fell across her bed, sobbing. She didn't answer her mother. Not until Rex returned home did Blanche learn what had happened.

"That boy, Gary, has the makings of a criminal, unless he really gets saved," Blanche said.

Charlene slept restlessly that night, so she arose later than usual Saturday morning, and was still in her pajamas, eating breakfast, when the phone rang. Blanche answered.

"It's for you, Charlene," her mother said. "Sounds like Gary."

"Gary? What's he calling me for?"

Charlene took her time in answering the phone for she wasn't too enthusiastic. "Hello," she said faintly.

"Charlene," Gary said, "there's one thing I want you to get straight. I'm not going to stand for you to date anyone but me, and if that Dick Holland ever takes you out again, I'll fix him for good."

"Why! Such nerve! Gary Streetland, who ever gave you the idea I was your steady? I'll go with whom I please."

"No, you won't. It's either me or no one, and if I can't have you, no one else's going to. Understand?"

Charlene exclaimed, "Gary Streetland, I want nothing to do with you, now or ever. You leave me alone!"

"You'll be sorry you said that," Gary said in a threatening tone of voice.

"I'm not afraid of you, Gary Streetland, and you needn't think you can bully me," Charlene said, her eyes snapping in anger. "Good-by!" she said as she slammed the receiver down.

"Charlene!" her mother cried. "I've never heard you talk to anyone like that. I'm surprised at you."

"I can't help it, Mother, that Gary seems to think he has a corner on me, and I refuse to be bluffed into being his steady, either now or ever. I can't stand that guy."

"But Charlene, don't you think it would have been wisdom to have handled him a little more graciously? Now he is apt to be angry, and there's no telling what he might do if you antagonize him. I'd much rather have him as my friend than as my enemy, for he could prove dangerous."

"He's not the kind who is willing to stop at being just a friend; and I'm not quite ready to marry anyone yet, let alone Gary."

"Well, finish your breakfast," Mother said.

"I'm not hungry now, Mother," Charlene replied, and went upstairs again.

CHAPTER 9

BLANCHE HAD THE BLUES. REX WAS PACKING HIS suitcase preparing to leave for Olean, New York, where he was to conduct two weeks revival meetings, and she stood by his side, helping him, primarily so she could be with him every moment until he departed. He had already hung his suits in the car and was now busy putting his other clothes in the suitcase. He never packed until he was ready to leave, and this worried Blanche no end, because she always spent two days packing before she took even a week-end trip to Philadelphia.

Rex looked up and saw how glum she looked, so he took hold of her chin, grinned and said, "Cheer up! It's only for two weeks. Anyone would think I was going away forever, the way you look."

"It will seem like forever to me," Blanche sighed. "I surely wish you didn't have to go; I'm sure some of the people in the church will not understand, because you haven't been here very long, you know."

"They never do understand, no matter how long you've been in a place, but they don't have to, for the work of the Lord must be carried on according to the guidance of the Holy Spirit, regardless of what people think or say."

"I just have a feeling you shouldn't go," Blanche said, and the worried look on her face caused Rex to hesitate.

"A woman and her feelings! I go by reason, not feelings."

"I know, but it is more than a feeling. I'm afraid of what may happen while you're away, for there's plenty of trouble brewing. I must confess, I haven't told you what's going on, because I didn't want to worry you while you are gone."

Rex stood upright and quit packing. "Now you do have me worried. Out with it, what's happened?"

"Oh, if I tell you, you'll be worried all the time you're gone. It'll wait until you get back."

"Blanche, it's my right to know, and you've never kept anything from me before. So, hurry up and tell me."

"Very well, I'll tell you. You know the old spinster, Miss Allsworth?"

"You mean the thin little lady who never gossips until she

makes you promise not to tell anyone what she's about to tell you because it's strictly . . ."

"That's her."

"And the real reason she wants you to swear to silence is so she will have a scoop on the dirty news?"

"Right!"

"And she always bemoans the fact that the world is in such a mess and wonders what it will all lead to, particularly the delinquency of the juveniles who hold hands and even sit next to each other?"

"Go on, finish it," Blanche said grinning. "She has black circles under her eyes and a long square chin and, yes, two feet with long pointed shoes."

"Well now, what does the oracle of prophecy say, both good and bad, mostly bad?"

"Rex, be serious. I know she's a talker, but sometimes it pays to listen to Dame Gossip to find out what's going on."

"I'm listening, so out with it; then I can finish packing. In the meantime, I'm breathless."

Blanche grinned and appeared somewhat relieved. "What's the use of telling you anything? Oh well, she phoned me last night and told me that Maggie Streetland is on the warpath. She's openly boasted that she'll ruin you if it's the last thing she ever does, and she insists it's for the good of the church, and her loyalty to the Lord demands it. She claims she has the goods on you and knows some things that'll ruin you if she tells them, which she threatens to do."

"Tell her to go ahead and do her worst if she gets any pleasure out of it, for I haven't any skeletons hanging in my closet to worry about, and if she can ruin me and my ministry, it should be done. Yes, sir, it should be done, right now."

"Rex, I know you haven't done anything to be ashamed of, but she can hurt you if she creates lies against you. She's already said you are sweet on her, and she's telling a story around that when she was in your office, you made advances toward her."

"Ha! Maggie Streetland? Could anyone go for that dame? How repulsive! The story is so ridiculous, no one would ever believe it. I'm glad that while she is at it, she's made her tale so outlandish it is utterly unreal and unbelievable. It's like a child saying he saw a thousand elephants jump over the back fence; no one ever believes it."

"She's still dangerous, Rex. She's the most cunning, shrewd, ruthless person I've ever known, and she's bent on ruining you."

"Tell me, Blanche, is there one person in the church who believes her foolish charges against me?"

"Just one, Deacon Wadsworth and his wife have been won over to her side. No one else that I know of."

"Even Deacon Wadsworth knows better; he's just found someone who will go along with him in attacking the preacher; he doesn't really believe her charges. He's as treacherous and disloyal as a cobra, and I'd expect him to do just what he has, because it's a part of his nature and he couldn't do different. Has anyone else fallen for her line?"

"No, of course not, but they are all talking, and she has the entire church upset. They are all like sheep that have been attacked by a wolf and are so bewildered they don't know what to do. They need your leadership now as never before."

Rex glanced at his watch. "Well, I don't have time to do anything about it now. I must leave if I'm to arrive in Olean in time to preach tonight, so I guess we'll just have to leave the problem in the hands of the Lord and let Him work it out. There isn't much I can do about it. I've always said, 'Never try to defend yourself when attacked, for your friends never need an explanation, and your enemies won't believe it anyway.'"

"You just go ahead and go; I don't want you to be late, but I warn you, as soon as you're gone, I'm going to trot myself right over to see that Maggie Streetland. No one's going to tell lies about my husband and get away with it. That's something I'm not going to stand for."

"Oh, no, you don't. You're no match for her. First thing you know, she'll be spreading tales about you, too. Furthermore, there's nothing to be gained by talking with Maggie Streetland, for that woman has never admitted a fault in her entire life. She'll turn the tables on you by making herself a martyr and the underdog who is being falsely accused by a monster, a jealous minister's wife. You can't win, arguing with her. You stay away from there, Blanche."

Blanche shook her head remorsefully. "If only you could be here this Sunday morning to bring this thing right out into the open and expose these lies before they spread too far."

"It wouldn't do any good; only make a martyr out of Maggie. The best thing is to forget about it and act as if nothing ever happened. Most troubles die out if you leave them alone."

"I have a feeling these won't."

"There you go. You and your feelings again."

"I still think they need some straight preaching. Don't these people realize they are wrecking their own church by repeating Maggie's gossip, and don't they know it is a malicious lie which she has purposely concocted just to ruin you because she is vindictive? It all began because her son, Gary, stole some money from the Sunday school, and you were gracious enough to pay it back out of your own pocket. Such a woman!"

"Blanche, let's not be naive. Preaching never changed anyone . . . only the Lord can do that, and then, only if they'll let Him. And people don't stop to think why Maggie is attacking me, nor do they consider the damage done by repeating her lies, even though they don't believe them, for their sole motive in talking is that they've been hurt, and, therefore, they squeal."

Rex closed his suitcase and dropped it on the floor. Putting his arms around Blanche, he kissed her good-by and patted her on the cheek. "Don't worry, dear. Everything will turn out all right. Time heals all wounds, and if we forget the whole thing, Maggie won't get anywhere. The entire bonfire she's lit will soon burn itself out."

Blanche laid her head on his shoulder and cried. "I'll miss you. I'll count the days until you return."

As Rex drove away, Blanche stood on the porch watching until his car disappeared in a cloud of dust, then she went inside and cried until she couldn't weep anymore.

As he traveled down the highway, Rex had time to think. *Where will this end? So many people in the valley need the Lord, and Satan is using that woman to keep them from being saved. And what will happen to Gary? I tremble when I think of his fate.*

He was behind a big coal truck now, and for a few minutes was too occupied driving to think. After passing the truck, he returned to his problem. "Lord, You'll have to handle this woman; I can't," he prayed. "But, please Lord, have mercy on her soul, and, somehow, save Gary if it be possible. Don't let her harm those innocent sheep in the little church."

Rex had a heavy heart that night when he entered the pulpit of the church in Olean. He couldn't forget the problem at home, and his burden seemed to increase instead of becoming lighter. The Lord gave him no peace until soon he began to realize that he must walk through the valley of the shadow of death before he would win the victory for which he prayed.

He thought of Gethsemane, the place where the Lord drank the dregs of the bitter cup of sorrow, and he was reminded that there was a time in each life when one must drink of the same cup. *It is inescapable,* he thought.

While Rex was conducting the meetings, Maggie Streetland spent most of her time on the telephone, or visiting the membership from door to door, endeavoring to poison the minds of the people against their new pastor. She was subtle. In prayer meeting she prayed for him, thanking God for such a wonderful pastor, but contrariwise, she called at the homes and carefully planted seeds of suspicion and hate.

At one home, Maggie said, "Well now, do tell me. Just what do you think of our new pastor?"

Before they could answer, she continued, "He's certainly a wonderful preacher, there's no getting around that fact, but he's about the smoothest talker I've ever heard; he'd deceive even the elect. The only trouble with him is, he tells everyone else what they ought to do, but he never applies it to himself.

"Do you know what I heard? You won't tell anyone if I tell you, now will you? Of course, you won't. I wouldn't want this to get out for anything, so we must all keep it absolutely quiet and confidential." Then Maggie leaned over and whispered, "I heard that in his last pastorate he was sweet on his secretary. Yes, indeed! In fact, that's why he had to leave. Well, now, I hated to tell you that, but then, I know you won't tell anyone and I think you should know about it."

Then Maggie leaned back in the chair and cackled, "Don't ask me exactly what it was all about, for I never did get the complete story. You see, I made a visit to his last church, just to check up and find out, but when they brought the subject up to me, I just clammed right up and refused to either listen or talk about the pastor. That's something I don't believe in doing. No, you'll never catch *me* gossiping.

"You just pray for him, won't you? He can never help us to God until he himself gets right with God; now can he?

"Oh, and there's another thing I almost forgot to tell you. He was asked to call on Mrs. Hadabaker, and he has never called yet. Of course, he must be busy. But don't you think I'm right when I say that a pastor ought to call on a person as sick as Mrs. Hadabaker? Poor soul! She might die. And then what?

"You won't tell anyone what I said, now will you? This is strictly confidential between us two."

Maggie had a way of keeping such slander confidential until she called at the next house.

Sunday, Deacon Wadsworth circulated a petition among the membership which read, "Inasmuch as we, the undersigned, feel that the pastor of the Radford Community Church, the Reverend Rex Brantford, is not competent; and inasmuch as he is neglecting the church work; and inasmuch as he is not spiritually qualified, we, the undersigned, feel it necessary to request his resignation, to take effect immediately."

Deacon Wadsworth was convinced that he would meet with ready response; however, as soon as he began to approach the people with the petition he met with so many rebuffs and rebukes, he withdrew it. Obviously, the people of the church weren't falling for the campaign.

"It may be a little premature to pass this petition," he concluded. Though he ceased circulating the petition, he was amazed to discover that he was growing steadily unpopular among the people.

"I just can't understand it. Why are people treating me the way they are?" Deacon Wadsworth complained. "It is evident that the pastor is turning all of my friends against me. It seems that people never do appreciate all that you've done for them; however, there's one comforting thought, God knows all about my faithful labors. He'll never forget me, even if the people do. I just can't understand it. Surely we are living in the last days." He shook his head mournfully.

CHAPTER 10

THE REVIVAL MEETING IN OLEAN, UNDER THE LEADERship and preaching of Rex Brantford, was beginning to gain momentum to such an extent that many were under deep conviction of sin and a few were accepting Christ. Many of the Christians of the church were being awakened from their spiritual lethargy as the Holy Spirit searched their hearts. Rex was convinced that a great revival was in the making and was confident that before the two weeks were finished, without a doubt, the entire community would be shaken for God.

He was terribly tired on that Tuesday night when he went

to bed, for he had been working in the inquiry room until midnight, counseling with those who were seeking salvation, but some of the friends had insisted that he drop over for some home-made ice cream, regardless of the late hour. Too weary to go, he tried to beg out of the engagement, but when he saw that he would offend them, he yielded and went.

When at last he finally went to the hotel and crawled into bed, he was too tired to relax, but after tossing restlessly for a long time, he did eventually fall asleep. He slept so soundly, he was entirely oblivious to his troubles and problems at the Radford Community Church which had bothered him so much.

It was early in the morning when the phone began to jangle repeatedly, but Rex was so exhausted, he didn't hear it. However, the phone rang so persistently, he finally awakened enough to pick up the receiver and answer, "Hello!"

"This is long distance, calling for Reverend Rex Brantford."

"Yes, this is Rex Brantford," he said.

Immediately, he heard Charlene say in an excited, emotional voice, "Oh, Daddy! Hurry home, just as fast as you can."

"Charlene! What's the matter? Tell me."

"I . . . I . . . just can't tell you, Daddy, it's too horrible, but Mother's dying. Get here as quickly as possible. Please hurry."

"Charlene . . ." She hung up.

Rex dressed as fast as he could. Tears blinded his eyes, and it seemed as if he couldn't tie his shoes or button his shirt. Everything went so slow it appeared that the entire world had suddenly conspired against him. The mystery of what had happened to Blanche preyed upon his mind until he thought he could not retain his equilibrium.

As soon as he had dressed, he ran down the hotel hall to the elevator and pushed the button continuously, but there was no response. *He's evidently asleep,* Rex thought. *I'll go down the service stairs,* but then he heard the cables moving, so he waited.

"Hurry!" he said as he stepped in the elevator.

"This thing doesn't move in a hurry," the combination bell-hop and elevator man replied. "If it did, it would probably break down. It's getting tired and old, just like me."

The idle chatter irritated Rex, but he contained his temper by remaining silent. It seemed the operator deliberately delayed opening the door when they reached the first floor, by jerking the elevator up and down until he had made a perfect landing. *Why doesn't he open that door?* Rex thought. At last he put his hand on the lever, smiled and said, "Well, we made it, didn't we? Sometimes I think old dolly'll expire and give up with one last, dying gasp."

Rex's cheeks were jerking nervously, and his eyes burned with irritation, despite his effort to control himself. He was about to say, "Will you please open that door?" when the old man at last leaned on the lever and it slowly opened. Before the process was finished, Rex had slipped through the opening and was gone.

"Well, I'll be . . . what's eatin' him, anyway?" the old man said as he slowly ambled to the overstuffed chair and prepared to resume sleeping.

The car had been sitting in the parking lot all night and wouldn't start. Rex paused long enough to pray, "Dear God, please help me." He touched the key again, and the motor coughed, then started, whereupon a cloud of black smoke came from the exhaust, indicating the carburator had been flooded.

He roared out of the parking lot and fortunately was not delayed with traffic at that early hour of the morning. He bit his lip impatiently as he swerved around the mountain curves. Finally, realizing he was psychologically unfit to drive a car, he deliberately slowed down, and, with much effort, exercised patience, lest he should have an accident.

Streaks of sunlight were painting the sky with long beams of yellow gold against a pink and purple background when Rex reached his mountain home. He dashed into the living room, calling, "Blanche, where are you?"

There was no answer, only a silence like death in a tomb, so he ran to their bedroom. It was empty, but when he went to Charlene's bedroom, he found the bed torn up, the furniture sprawled upon the floor, the rug kicked up, and . . . there it was! Blood splattered on the rug and smeared on the wall!

"Oh God," he prayed, "what's happened? It can't be."

"Charlene!" he called.

No answer.

He ran to the kitchen, and there on the breakfast table was a note in Charlene's handwriting: "I've gone to the hospital in Port Allegheny to be with mother. Come as quickly as you can. Charlene."

It took Rex only thirty-five minutes to drive the thirty miles to the hospital, but when he arrived, it seemed the receptionist took as long as she could to inform him which room Blanche was in.

The elevator was on the top floor, so he didn't wait for it, but instead ran up the stairs to the second floor.

A sign on the door read No Visitors, but he rushed in and there he saw her, bruised and swollen, pale as a piece of chalk. He thought she was dead.

"Blanche," he cried.

"You . . . you've come. I . . . didn't think you'd make it," she said. "I thought I'd die before you got here."

"No, Blanche, you aren't going to die. God won't let you die; I'm going to pray for you. You mustn't talk like that."

"I'm not afraid to die. You'll take good care of Charlene, won't you?"

"Of course, but you're going to get well, Blanche. I need you, and God knows it. Fight to live; don't give up."

He kissed her gently; she slowly ran her fingers through his hair. "I'm sorry you had to come home," she said.

She closed her eyes again and became unconcious.

Rex motioned Charlene to go outside the room with him, and as soon as they were outside the door, he asked, "Charlene, tell me, what's happened."

"Daddy, last night, I was awakened by a strange sound in my room. In the moonlight, I saw a figure steal across the room toward me. I saw the flash of a knife blade as he passed the window, and when I saw it, I screamed and jumped from the bed, just as he tried to stab me. I'm sure he would have killed me, had it not been for the fact that Mother heard my scream and came to my aid. In the dark, she grappled with the prowler and tried to fight him off, but he was too strong for her, and finally he drove the knife into her breast, just below her right shoulder. She fell to the floor, and he fled, disappearing in the bushes back of the house."

"Were you able to see who it was? Did you recognize him?"

"No, it was too dark. We haven't the faintest idea of his identity. The police came right over, and the only clues they seem to have located so far are a few strands of hair which mother pulled from his head when she was struggling with him. They looked for finger prints, but found none. They also took the bedroom scatter rugs to their laboratory to look for clues."

"What did the doctor say about Mother's condition? Do they think she will be all right?"

"They didn't say much, and my impression was that they don't hold much hope for her."

The tears welled up in Rex's eyes. He shook his head in grief but tried to hide his sorrow.

"Why would anyone want to harm us?" he pondered. "What have we done to deserve such hate and why would anyone wish to kill you, a sweet, innocent Christian girl who's never hurt anyone?"

He returned to Blanche's bedside where he knelt and prayed for her. After a while, he heard a faint whisper, "I love you."

"And I love you, too," Rex said affectionately. He arose from his knees and kissed her. Looking up, he saw the doctor standing beside him. "Oh, hello, Doctor. I didn't see you come in. How is she, Doctor?"

"We'll just check her and see," the doctor answered evasively. After checking the blood transfusion, he took her blood pressure again, and then listened to her heart through his stethoscope. "You're doing just fine," he said casually. "Just keep fighting and you'll be all right." Turning to Rex he said, "May I see you at the desk, please? There are papers you should fill out."

Doctor John Holiday was a fairly young man, tall, thin, and pleasant, but serious. He was dressed casually but neatly. Whenever he entered the hospital, the nurses brightened up and even the patients became more cheerful as they heard him coming down the hall, for he was like sunshine in January. He was an optimist, therefore Rex knew, having met him during his hospital visitation, that he would view Blanche's condition from a favorable viewpoint, so he could expect the brightest report possible.

"Reverend," he said as he walked toward the desk, "your wife is in a most critical condition, and from the human viewpoint, there isn't too much hope; however, with your prayers and God's help, there is a chance for her recovery. The next three days will tell the story."

"Then her condition is serious?" Rex suggested.

"Yes. Extremely so; I don't believe in misrepresenting the case to you. However, I repeat, I am most hopeful, knowing that you are a man of prayer and that God can intervene, but I wish to be emphatic in saying that if she does recover, it'll be the work of God and not any skill of mine that will be responsible."

"I appreciate your honesty, Doctor. Now I'll know how to pray."

"Exactly. There is one thing you can do to help, if you will."

"What is that, Doctor?"

"We need blood donors to replace the blood we've used from the blood bank, and there will be a need for much more."

"I'll give blood, Doctor, and I'll also ask members of the church to make donations. I'm sure they'll respond readily."

"Thank you." The doctor left in haste.

Rex returned to Blanche's room, and Charlene, who had been sitting quietly in the chair in the corner of the room, looked up inquiringly.

Rex shook his head negatively, and Charlene wiped tears from her eyes.

"What did the doctor say?" Blanche asked weakly.

"You are doing as good as can be expected," Rex said truthfully. "With prayer, you'll come through all right. Have faith in God, Blanche; He has never failed us yet, and He won't forsake us now."

Blanche smiled sweetly and fell asleep.

Both Rex and Charlene remained with her throughout the day and the night, returning to the manse the following morning for breakfast.

"Charlene," Rex said, "I think you should get some rest, so why don't you go to bed and sleep until noon, and I'll pick you up after lunch? Agreeable?"

"I want to be with Mother," Charlene answered.

"I can understand that, but you must get some sleep or you'll be sick. You can't take too much of this."

"How about you, Daddy?"

"I'm more used to getting along without sleep. I'll make out all right. Besides, I can sleep sitting up in the chair. Now be sure all the doors are locked while I'm away, and don't answer the door bell for anyone. I don't like to leave you here alone, but under the circumstances, I have no choice."

Rex phoned the pastor of the church in Olean and informed him he would not be able to return to continue the meetings for at least three more days, possibly more, and urged him to get another minister to take his place and to continue the meetings until he could leave Blanche.

CHAPTER 11

As DOCTOR HOLIDAY PREDICTED, BLANCHE'S CONDItion remained extremely critical for three days, but she began to improve slowly on the fourth day.

Rex didn't go to bed during those three days, but snatched a few moments of sleep sitting in the chair, whenever he could.

Charlene remained at home evenings after arrangements had been made for one of the church members to stay with her, and she returned to school, visiting the hospital each evening.

On the fourth morning, Doctor Holiday said to Rex, "I think it would be safe for you to go home and get some much needed sleep. First thing you know, you'll be cracking up and we'll have you in the hospital, too, if you don't get some rest."

"I'm worried about him," Blanche said weakly. "He's been so faithful."

"If you're sure everything will be all right, I think I'll take your advice," Rex agreed. "You won't mind, will you, Blanche?" He kissed her and patted her cheek affectionately. "Be good till I get back this afternoon."

When Rex reached home, he was so exhausted, he fell across the bed without undressing and immediately went to sleep. About three o'clock there was an insistent pounding at the front door, but at first Rex didn't hear it. However, the knocking continued persistently until he was finally aroused. Rubbing his eyes, he slowly arose, wondering what could have happened to justify such insistent pounding. When he was more fully awake, he hurried to the door and opened it. It was Deacon Wadsworth.

"Sorry to awaken you in the middle of the day . . . you were sleeping, weren't you? You must have been. It must be great to be a preacher and be able to sleep in the daytime when the rest of us have to work." A bitter-sweet grin masked the true sarcasm of the man's thought.

"Come in," Rex said without making any explanation in self-defense. "What can I do for you, Brother Wadsworth?"

"Pastor, there are many whisperings floating around about you, and though I don't believe them, nevertheless, I thought it best to go right to headquarters and get the story firsthand. Just what are the true facts of the case?"

"What case?"

"Why, the accusations Mrs. Streetland is making against you. I think the public is due an answer."

"Just what do you wish to know, Deacon? Maybe I can set your mind at ease."

"Well, Maggie Streetland claims you won't even talk with her and face the charges she is making; don't you think it would be advisable for you to face her and answer her accusations?"

"She's never asked to see me in the first place, and furthermore, I don't know what charges she is making, so if you'll enlighten me, I'll be most happy to tell you whether they are true."

"She claims that you had to leave your former pastorate because of an affair you had with your secretary."

"On what information does she base such a charge?"

"She visited your former parish and inquired about you, so she says."

"That is her privilege, but obviously, she went looking for trouble, and I'm sure she could find someone in that community who wasn't loyal to the pastor, for there are such people in every community who gossip and spread falsehoods; however, if she had talked to the reputable leaders of the church, she would have discovered that my reputation has never been marred. Her accusations, if she has made such a charge, are absolutely false and unfounded."

"Is it true you have been accusing her of lying about you?"

"No, though I'm beginning to believe it."

"Pastor, I think you're due her a public apology, and I think you should humble yourself and face her charges, answering them to the satisfaction of all concerned."

"Deacon, I have no apologies to make, for I've done nothing against her, and any apology I might make would be an admission of guilt when I'm not at fault. I see no value in airing her slanders against me by making any public statement."

"I think you should."

"And I think I shouldn't."

"It's too bad, Pastor. Your attitude is certainly not becoming to the ministry, and I think you should show more charity toward this poor soul whom you are treading beneath your feet."

"Now, just a minute. That isn't true! I'm not treading her beneath my feet, and I've never said or done anything against her. On the other hand, I've patiently remained silent while she has been spreading lies against me and have said nothing in self-defense, because I'm convinced a righteous person needs make no defense against false charges."

"Sooner or later, Pastor, you'll have to make an explanation to the public, whether you like it or not." Deacon Wadsworth reached for his hat and said, "I guess I might as well be going; there's no use talking with you."

"Come again, Deacon," Rex said as he closed the door behind him.

Rex went to the kitchen, put on a pot of coffee, and started frying bacon and eggs. He dropped a couple of pieces of toast in the toaster and quickly set the table. *It's a funny time of day to be cooking breakfast,* he thought, *but Charlene will be home from school soon, and we'll go to the hospital. She can fix what she likes.*

There was another knock at the door, so he set the frying pan aside and went to answer it.

"Why come in, Mrs. Hagood," he said. "I was just cooking some breakfast. Came home from the hospital early this morning and slept until now, so it's a rather late breakfast, wouldn't you say?"

"Yes, it must be a great strain on you, Pastor. How is your wife? We're all so concerned about her and praying for her."

"She's slightly improved," Rex said. "I wish I could say she's entirely out of danger, but that wouldn't be truthful. Won't you sit down? Here, let me take your coat."

"Pastor," Mrs. Hagood began, "I didn't come to gossip or to add to your burdens, but I wondered if you knew about the talk that's going on in the church?"

Rex looked at the kindly old lady, a widow for many years. She was dressed in clothing which was well kept but old and outdated, and wore a shawl which was wrapped about her head and neck. She removed it and folded it neatly before laying it on the table. Next, she set her large black pocketbook on the floor beside her.

She is one of the innocents who is being hurt, he thought.

"I've heard a few things, Mrs. Hagood," he replied, "but probably not as much as you have, though really, it doesn't matter. I wouldn't worry about it, if I were you."

"But, Pastor, it hurts me when people say such things against you, because I know you're a man of God, and it just isn't fair to add to your burdens at a time like this. I don't know what you can do about it, for that woman — you know whom I mean — can't be shut up, but something ought to be done to silence her. I just wondered if you knew what was being said?"

"Yes, Mrs. Hagood, but there isn't a word of truth in what she says, and you mustn't let it bother you."

"But aren't you planning to answer her and to . . . well, deal with that woman? I think she should be put out of the church."

"No, Mrs. Hagood. We mustn't do that. We'll go right ahead loving people and preaching Christ in all of His goodness and love; somehow, our critics must learn that God is love, and they'll never realize it unless we return good for evil. If I should start fighting back, then I'd be as bad as they are; so I must overcome evil with good and not be overcome with evil by duplicating their mistakes, or by becoming vindictive."

Mrs. Hagood began to cry. "Why do people have to act like this? Why can't we worship God in our little church without someone stirring up trouble all the time? Church isn't a place to fight; it's a place to learn the love of God, and if we're going to fuss and fight all the time, then there's no point in going to church at all. Oh, I just don't understand it."

"I agree with you, Mrs. Hagood, and you're so right, but there isn't much we can do about it, for people will be people, and we can't wish them into being what they should be when they're not. It's best to forget the whole thing, refuse to think about it or to repeat it. Tell it to the Lord and go on serving Him."

"I guess you're right," she said as she wrapped her shawl about her neck and gathered up her things, getting ready to leave.

"Come again," Rex said as she walked slowly down the steps.

Soon after, Charlene arrived on the school bus and ran into the house. "Daddy, I'm home."

"That's good," he said. "Come to the kitchen and get what you want to eat, so we can go to the hospital as soon as possible. I'm cooking bacon and eggs for myself."

"Cook some for me, too, Daddy. That sounds good."

"All right," he said as he broke two additional eggs into the pan and added a couple of strips of bacon.

"Daddy, the phone's ringing. Shall I answer it?"

"Please do," he said. *I wonder who wants to talk over the trouble Maggie is stirring up now,* Rex thought. *Don't I have enough trouble without having all this mess heaped on me? That woman is so busy stirring up fusses, I don't have time to straighten them out, and if she isn't doing anything else, she's wasting my valuable time until I'm almost at the breaking point.*

"It's the doctor," Charlene said.

Rex dropped the spatula and hurried to the phone. "Yes, Doctor."

"Reverend, you'd better come to the hospital at once."

"What's wrong?"

"I don't like to say it, but your wife has suddenly taken a turn for the worse. I can't understand it, for she was doing so well, but all at once, she is utterly exhausted, her blood pressure has gone way down and her pulse rate is way too weak. Besides, she seems emotionally upset about something and cries all the time."

"Thanks, Doctor. I'll come immediately." He ran to the

kitchen, took the frying pan from the stove and said, "Charlene, we haven't time to eat. Something's happened to Mother. She's taken a turn for the worse."

They drove as fast as they dared to the hospital and hurried to Blanche's room. They found her sobbing and crying hysterically.

"Blanche! What's the matter?" Rex asked.

She couldn't answer but continued sobbing and gasping for breath.

"Blanche, you must stop crying. Tell me. What's wrong?"

"It's . . . it's what Maggie's saying about you."

"Maggie? What's she saying? Who told you?"

"Janie . . . Sears . . . was here . . . she told . . . me . . ." Blanche burst into a new spasm of crying.

"Now, Blanche, you mustn't let it upset you so. No one can hurt me, not as long as God is on my side. Now tell me, what did she say?"

"She . . . said . . . Maggie's . . . accused you . . . of making advances . . . to her . . . in your office."

"Oh, sweetheart, that's so preposterous, and no one'll believe it. Who'd ever want to make advances to that . . . oh well, I won't say it. But you mustn't let this silly talk upset you. You know it isn't so."

"I know it, but . . . I just can't take it . . . when . . . I'm so weak. I can't . . . help . . . but . . . cry."

"Blanche, you must forget it and stop worrying. I'm not letting it worry me, and you mustn't pay any attention to it either. Hasn't God promised He will never leave us nor forsake us? And if God be for us, who can be against us? So rest in the Lord. You mustn't cry like this, for it isn't good for you and if you're to get well, you must forget your cares and rest in the Lord."

Blanche's face brightened and she tried to smile. "I'll be all right, now. I just had to have you to help me. I'm so weak."

Rex kissed her. "There now. You close your eyes and go to sleep. Let the Lord carry your burdens, like He told you He would, for you are too weak and you need Him to be your burden bearer."

"Kiss me again," she said.

Rex kissed her and pulled the blanket about her shoulder. She fell asleep from sheer exhaustion.

Rex tiptoed from the room and found the doctor down the hall. "Doctor," he said, "please order a 'No Visitor' sign to be put on the door again, and order the nurses to enforce it, strictly, not allowing anyone other than Charlene and myself to enter the room, except the nurses."

"Why? What's happened?"

"Some well-meaning but foolish person visited Blanche this afternoon and upset her with the church troubles."

"They may have been well-meaning, but it could cost her life," Doctor Holliday said. "I'll order the sign up immediately, and we'll give her a sedative."

"Thank you," Rex said and tiptoed back into the room. He and Charlene sat silently watching as she slept fitfully. As Rex thought over the events of the afternoon, and what Maggie's gossip was doing to Blanche, he became increasingly angry. *They have no idea what they're doing*, he thought, *but I wonder if Maggie'd care even if she did know, for she's only interested in herself.*

CHAPTER 12

REX AND CHARLENE LEFT THE HOSPITAL LATE THAT night after Blanche appeared to be some better. She relaxed after Rex reassured her.

About nine o'clock the following morning, soon after Charlene had left for school, a state police car stopped in front of the parsonage, and Rex saw two policemen come to the door.

"Come in," he invited them.

"Thank you, sir. We would like to talk with you, if you don't mind," one of them said.

"Certainly," Rex replied. "Won't you be seated?"

"Thank you. Reverend Brantford, I'm sure you know why we're here. This is a strange case, and though we've been tracing down every clue, and there are a few, we are at a loss to understand the motive for the attack on your daughter and wife. Maybe you can help us."

"I'll be glad to assist in any way possible," Rex replied.

"Reverend Brantford, do either you, your wife, or daughter, have any known enemies who might have reason to wish to harm you? Obviously, the prowler who attacked your wife was intent on doing bodily harm to your daughter. There must have been some provocative incident to cause him to go to such extreme measures, and he must have been either angry, or else deeply grieved, to commit such an act."

"No, none of us have any enemies, so far as I know. I'm as puzzled as you," Rex said. He frowned in concentration. "The whole thing seems so preposterous and fantastic, I've wondered a thousand times why anyone would seek to do us harm when all we've ever done is good, and our whole life is devoted to helping others."

"That may be true, but there are some strange people in this world. Either someone, who is probably supersensitive, has misunderstood your motive, or else he's been unintentionally grieved by something either you, or your wife, or your daughter have said or done, though you may have never intended to offend him. Such a person could still prove to be dangerous, both to you and your family and to the community in general. He should be apprehended."

Rex hesitated, *I don't like to accuse either Maggie Streetland or Gary,* he thought. *They're members of the church, and I don't want to get them into trouble.*

The policeman noticed his hesitancy, so he said, "Reverend, I know you're in an embarrassing position, and you don't like to accuse anyone, but let me assure you that whatever you say will be kept in strictest confidence, and we'll be careful not to betray you. We merely want a lead to any clues which might guide us to investigate the guilty person. We wouldn't want him to have even an inkling of our suspicion, otherwise our investigations would be hampered."

"I see," Rex said thoughtfully. "I think I should tell you, then, about a situation in the church, but, gentlemen, I'd never in this world suspect any of my people as being guilty of so ruthless a crime. The idea's almost fantastic!"

"You never know, Reverend," the policeman said. "In our business we suspect everyone. When people go berserk, they do strange things, and sometimes the people you suspect the least are the very ones who do crazy things."

"Well, I expect you to keep this in the strictest confidence," Rex began. "There is one woman in the church who has vowed to ruin me, namely, Mrs. Maggie Streetland. She is spreading the most preposterous tales and doing everything in her power to harm me and force me to leave my pulpit."

"Why does she wish to do you harm?"

"I wish I knew. It may be vengeance because her son was in a little scrape and I had to deal with him. I actually defended him, but probably when he told the story to her, he painted it up to shield himself and place the blame on me."

"Hmmm. Could you tell us the details of this problem with her son?"

"I'd rather not go into details if you don't mind. Somewhat confidential, I'd say."

"Is this Mrs. Streetland normal psychologically?"

"I don't like to say. My opinion is that she is highly emotional."

"And her son, what's his name? Is he a normal boy?"

"His name is Gary. He's somewhat of a trouble maker. His mother has always protected him and spoiled him somewhat."

"Has he ever paid any particular attention to your daughter?"

"Yes, he has. He's very possessive and extremely jealous. He did threaten her if she paid attention to anyone else, but the whole idea is ridiculous, for she has never so much as had a date with him, and she dislikes him in the extreme."

"He may have had his feelings hurt then?"

"Probably, but I never take young people's crushes too seriously. It doesn't amount to anything."

"It may be more serious than you think, Reverend. We'll keep this information in confidence, as we promised, but you have been most helpful, and we thank you."

"Really, I don't think I'd waste time investigating either Gary or his mother, gentlemen. They'd never do anything so wicked as to try to kill anyone. A few words of gossip and some underhanded schemes would be the limit of their capability to do wrong."

"You're sure you have no other enemies?"

"To my knowledge, no."

"Thank you, sir. We'll keep you posted if we discover anything of interest. Good day, sir."

"Come again. I'll do anything I can to help," Rex said.

Rex looked at his watch and thought, *I'll have to hurry to the hospital.* He put on his hat and coat and was leaving when the phone rang. At first he hesitated, then thought, *It might be something important. I'd better answer.*

"Hello, Reverend Brantford speaking," he said.

"Reverend, I must see you right away. Will you be home?"

"I was just leaving for the hospital, but if it's that urgent I can wait. What did you wish to see me about?"

"I must talk with you."

"Could you give me an idea about what's troubling you?

Maybe it's something we could discuss on the phone and save you a trip to the parsonage."

"Oh no, I wouldn't want to talk about it on the phone. Not this. I'll say just this much; Maggie Streetland is saying some terrible things about you, and I think you ought to know. Also, I, myself, want to know the real facts."

Rex groaned. *Here we go again,* he thought. "Sister, that will take a little time, and I must leave for the hospital at once, so how about seeing me here at the parsonage immediately after dinner? Would that be all right?"

"I wanted to see you now, but I guess it can wait if you can't see me now."

"I'll see you about one o'clock, then." Rex hung up and left before the phone could ring again.

That woman, Maggie Streetland, he thought. *Why doesn't she choke herself to death talking so much? I've had just about enough from her.* Though he wasn't serious in his thoughts, he was extremely angry.

He found Blanche slightly improved, but her recovery had definitely been retarded by worry. Rex was experiencing an increased battle within his inner soul. It was not easy to control his smoldering temper when he saw Blanche being hurt.

CHAPTER 13

BLANCHE IMPROVED SLOWLY. FOUR DAYS LATER, Doctor Holliday came into her hospital room when Rex was there and said, "Reverend, this young lady is doing all right. She's going to make it, but for a time, she had us all scared. She's come out of the woods now and I'm glad to say she's out of danger."

"That's wonderful news, Doctor!" Rex exclaimed. "You've certainly done a wonderful job, and we deeply appreciate what you've done."

"Don't thank me. Thank the Lord, for He's the One who has saved her life. Without God, we physicians would be helpless."

"I agree," Rex said, "but God also used your skill, just as He uses my messages to save souls. You're due some credit."

"No, not me, not in this case. But for the goodness of God, your wife wouldn't be here."

"The reason God can use you, Doctor, is because you're so humble," Blanche said with a smile.

Doctor Holliday shook his head. "Reverend," he said, "it would now be safe for you to return to your meeting in Olean if you wish."

"Why don't you, Rex?" Blanche urged. "I'll be all right. I think it would be wonderful if you could be with them for this closing week-end."

"I guess I will," Rex said. "At any rate, I'll have to go back to the hotel and pick up my clothes which I forgot when I left in such a hurry. I'll phone the pastor and see what he says."

"He'll want you," Blanche said.

"You're sure you'll be all right?"

"Of course," she answered.

Rex left Friday afternoon and took Charlene with him, for he didn't wish to leave her home alone.

Upon their return Monday, Rex found Blanche decidedly improved. She had gained much strength, and her recovery was assured.

"The doctor says I may be able to go home the first of next week, unless I should suffer a set-back," Blanche announced.

"Wonderful!" Rex said. "I'm proud of you."

Charlene more and more took over the burdens of the housework. Each afternoon, upon returning home from school, she would cook the dinner, wash the dishes and then do her school work.

When Rex told Blanche about her faithfulness, she said, "She's a wonderful girl. I can't bring myself to think what it would have been like if she had been killed that night; it's too dreadful to consider. Why would anyone want to harm her?"

"It's hard to comprehend," Rex said.

Friday afternoon of that week, while riding home on the school bus, Dick Holland reminded Charlene, "Tomorrow morning is the opening day of hunting season, and I hope you haven't forgotten your promise to go grouse hunting with me."

"Oh, but Dick, Mother is sick and in the hospital, and I'm afraid Daddy wouldn't be able to go, not now at least, not until she comes home."

"Couldn't we go out just for the morning, and he could go to the hospital in the afternoon?"

"I'll ask him and see what he says. I'll phone you."

"All right. Thanks, Charlene."

As soon as Charlene arrived home, she ran excitedly into the house, looking for her father, but he wasn't home yet, so she started preparing supper.

Soon after, the phone rang. *That must be Dick,* she thought. "Hello!" she said.

"Charlene, this's Gary. I heard Dick ask you to go hunting tomorrow. I'm warning you not to go."

"Gary, you tend to your own business and I'll tend to mine," she said saucily.

"I'm giving you fair warning. I told you, if I can't have you, no one will."

Charlene hung up without answering him. *He makes me good and tired,* Charlene thought.

Supper was almost ready when Rex returned from the hospital and from making other sick calls. Charlene heard him coming and met him at the door.

"Oh, Daddy, guess what? Tomorrow is the opening day of hunting season and Dick wants us to go out with him. I told him I doubted if you could go, because you must visit Mother, but he said maybe you could go just for the morning."

"Well now, I might just do that. Your mother is so much better, I think if I told her when I see her tonight what we plan to do, she'd be in favor of it."

"Oh good! May I phone Dick, then, and make it definite?"

"Sure, go ahead. I'm anxious for you to shoot that gun. Who knows? You might accidentally hit something." Rex grinned.

"I'll show you I can shoot that gun; I've been practicing."

Charlene quickly phoned Dick. "Dick? This's Charlene. Daddy says we can go. What time will you be here?"

"Just before nine o'clock. The season doesn't open till nine."

"We'll be looking for you."

Charlene left the phone and put supper on the table.

As they sat down to eat supper, Charlene said, "Daddy, I'm so excited, I just can't wait."

"You deserve to have a good time," he said.

"Gary heard Dick ask me to go hunting, and he phoned soon after I was home and warned me not to go. If he thinks he can bluff me, he's wrong."

"You say Gary phoned?"

"Yes, Gary. He seems to think he has a corner on me."

Rex said nothing, but began to ponder the implications of his threat. *Could he be so warped psychologically that he could be the prowler who came the other night? Oh, that's impossible,* he thought, and shrugged off the thought. *Yet, the police said you could never exclude anyone as a suspect, for people do strange things when they are emotionally upset.*

"A penny for your thoughts, Daddy," Charlene said. "You look so serious."

"Oh, me? I have my pensive moments. Let's have some more of that gravy; it's good. You're a good cook, Charlene."

"Do you really think so, Daddy?" Charlene asked. Her face revealed her pleasure at his compliment.

The next morning, Dick arrived on schedule and said, "It's so cold, windy and blustery, I think the grouse will likely be hiding in the valley in the hemlock trees along the creek, so let's walk carefully down the stream toward my place. I'll go in the middle and you can walk on either side to shoot them when I flush them."

"That isn't fair," Rex said.

"I'll get my share. I'll see 'em sitting."

They hadn't gone far before a bird flushed from a hemlock and zoomed around the trees on Charlene's side. She shot and missed.

"I'm sure I hit him," she said.

"If you'd hit him, he'd have come down, but never mind, a lot better shots than we are, miss 'em," Rex said.

Shortly afterward, Dick saw one sitting near the trunk of a tree, about three quarters of the way up, and shot it.

"That isn't fair," Charlene said. "You shot him sitting."

"That's about the only way I can get 'em," Dick confessed, "but it isn't everyone who can see 'em sitting."

When they had gone as far as Dick's house, he shot another grouse and had his limit of birds. "Now it's up to you to shoot 'em, because I can't shoot any more," Dick said.

"They make me so mad," Charlene said. "I can't hit any of them."

While she was talking, another bird flushed. Rex shot him. "That's one for me," he said.

As he was picking it up, he accidentally flushed another bird, and being caught off guard, it was gone before he could shoot, but someone shot from the opposite direction, barely missing Charlene.

"What's the idea?" Rex called angrily. "Who shot toward us?"

"I didn't see you," the person answered, and Rex looked up and saw Gary Streetland standing there with a sour expression, his nose twitching with disdain.

"What's the matter with you?" Rex scolded. "Are you blind?

Anyone in their right mind would know we were here. Didn't you hear me?"

"Are you accusing me of intentionally trying to shoot Charlene?" Gary sneered.

"I'm saying you're dangerous in the woods, and if you don't have any better sense than you have just demonstrated, you shouldn't be allowed to have a gun."

Both Dick and Charlene remained silent until Gary turned and disappeared in the forest, then Charlene said, "Daddy, that was no accident. I think he really wanted to hurt me."

"We can't prove that, Charlene, but I do think we'd better hunt back toward our house; there's no use antagonizing him any further."

"If you ask me, Reverend Brantford, I think it's time somebody had a showdown with Gary, and I think I'll call his bluff."

"No, Dick, better leave him alone, for nothing's to be gained by a fight. Come on, let's hunt toward home."

No more grouse were shot that morning, and when they arrived at the house, Dick insisted on giving his birds to Charlene.

"I'll accept them under one condition only," Charlene said. "You must be our guest for Sunday dinner, tomorrow, and help us eat them. Will you come?"

Dick grinned broadly. "Sure," he said.

CHAPTER 14

IT WAS ALMOST TWO O'CLOCK BEFORE CHARLENE HAD dinner on the table Sunday afternoon, despite the fact that Rex and Dick both assisted her in setting the table, peeling the potatoes and performing other kitchen chores.

The grouse were delicious, prepared the same way her mother cooked chicken. After rolling them in flour, she fried them to a crisp brown, and then covered them with water and allowed them to simmer slowly until they were so tender the meat fell from the bones. She made gravy with the remaining broth and, as always, she mashed the potatoes because they were her favorite dish.

"You're some cook!" Rex complimented her.

"I'll say," Dick agreed. "Anyone would think you'd been cooking for the last fifty years; your cooking's just as good as Mom's."

"Are you sure you aren't just teasing me?" Charlene asked.

"No, we're not," Rex said. "Give me some more of those potatoes and gravy . . . Dick, help yourself first."

"Don't mind if I do," Dick said and dished out another big plateful.

"Mother comes home tomorrow, Dick," Charlene said. "I'm so happy I don't know what to do with myself. It's been pretty lonesome around here."

"That's swell," Dick agreed. "I 'spose she'll take over when she gets back and you'll have a rest for a change?"

"On the contrary," Rex said, "Charlene'll be busier than ever, cooking for her too. It'll be a while before Mother'll be able to do anything, and we'll have to safeguard her against any worries or problems whatsoever."

Charlene had baked a chocolate cake the night before, so she cut generous pieces and served it with pineapple for dessert.

"Uhmmm," Rex marveled as he bit into the cake. "This's great."

Just then, he heard a car stop in front of the house, and someone ran onto the front porch and banged frantically on the door. Whoever it was, he left the engine running and the car door open.

"Sounds like trouble," Rex said solemnly. "Wonder what's up now?" He dropped his fork and hurried to the door.

"Brother Leighton, come in! Something wrong?"

"Yes, Pastor. It's Danny Bosworth. He's been shot."

"Danny? Shot? Why, I just saw him in Sunday school. How did this happen?"

"He went over to Streetlands to play with Sonny Streetland after dinner, and the two of them went to the basement and found Gary's revolver lying on the work bench. Sonny unintentionally pointed it at Danny and it went off."

"Where is Danny, and how is he?"

"His condition is serious, Pastor, and they've rushed him to the hospital, but I'm afraid they'll never make it in time, he was bleeding so profusely. Shot in the lower right side, they said."

"I'll hurry over immediately," Rex said. Turning to Dick he requested, "Dick, would you be kind enough to stay with Charlene until I return? I don't like to leave her alone, not after what happened."

"Sure, I'd be glad to, Reverend Brantford," Dick said.

Rex left without further delay. On the way, he trembled to think of the feud this accident might set forth in the valley where everyone was related in some way, and all felt duty bound to avenge their own by killing a relative of the deceased in order to square the

score. Hate was the law of the land, and honor demanded retri-
bution.

He thought of Sonny Streetland and trembled at the danger
the boy faced and the prospects a small lad, only twelve, faced at
the hands of determined, ruthless and vindictive relatives.

"Where is Danny Bosworth?" he inquired as he entered the
hospital.

"He's still in the emergency room," he was told.

Rex hurried down the hall to emergency, and there he found
Danny, pale and dying.

"Hello, Reverend Brantford," he said weakly. "Thanks for
coming."

Rex took the lad's hand in his own and said, "Danny, I'm so
sorry. I'll pray for you."

"I don't want to die," he said.

"And we don't want you to die, Danny. Tell me how it happened."

"It wasn't Sonny's fault, honest it wasn't. We were playing with
the gun, and it just went off. He didn't mean to do it; he's my best
friend. Please don't let them blame Sonny."

"We'll try to explain it to them, Danny. Now you mustn't
talk too much, for you must save your strength, so let's pray."

Danny closed his eyes in prayer, and Rex prayed for both
Danny and Sonny. "Sonny must feel awful about this, Lord,"
Rex prayed, "so please forgive him and comfort him just now."

When Rex had finished praying, Danny asked, "Would you
please go see Sonny and tell him I'm not mad at him? He didn't
mean to do it; I know he didn't."

"Yes, Danny, I'll go."

"Thanks," he said, and his eyes seemed to set. Tears came
into Rex's eyes as he looked at the freckle-faced boy who wouldn't
have a chance to live his life, and he held his hand until he felt
the pulse slowly grow weaker, faster and, at last, it finally ceased.
The nurse closed his eyelids and pulled the sheet over his face.

"He's gone," Rex said to his parents who stood nearby. "I'm
sorry."

"Oh, Brother Brantford, he isn't dead, is he? He can't be.
He'll get well, won't he?" Mrs. Bosworth sobbed.

"No, I'm afraid not. He's already with Jesus, even now, Mrs.
Bosworth; he's in heaven."

"Come on, Sue," Frank Bosworth said as he put his arm

around her and led her away. Then he paused and said, "Reverend Brantford, would you do us a favor?"

Rex pitied them; they were so poor and helpless, his heart was deeply moved. Mrs. Bosworth was a poorly dressed woman, slightly on the heavy side, and weather beaten by many years of hardship and unending work. Her husband was a medium-sized man whose face was drawn and harsh after years of valiantly fighting against odds to support his family. He was strong, having spent most of his life cutting logs and hauling them from the mountain to be used for braces in the coal mines of central Pennsylvania.

"What would you like for me to do?" Rex asked.

"I heard your first sermon about forgiving our enemies, and . . ." his voice quavered, "I was trying to say, I'm glad I heard it before this happened, otherwise I wouldn't have forgiven Sonny, but now I know he couldn't help it and didn't mean to harm Danny, so I wish you'd go over to the Streetlands with us to see Sonny like Danny asked just before he died. I want to forgive him."

"Of course," Rex agreed. "You go ahead and I'll meet you there."

Rex had hoped to visit Blanche while at the hospital, but when he had considered the situation more carefully, he concluded it was better this way, for it was unwise to tell Blanche what had happened.

On the way to the Streetlands, he wondered what Maggie would do when she saw him, but this thought did not deter him in the least, because he was on a mission of mercy. *If it weren't for the Gospel of Jesus Christ, another feud with its useless bloodshed would have already begun*, he thought.

When he reached the Streetland home, the Bosworths had already arrived and were waiting for him. They went to the front door together and knocked. At first they thought no one was at home, then the door opened slowly. It was the first time Rex had met Jake Streetland, and he was shocked. The little, mousy man appeared to be just the opposite to Maggie, and he couldn't quite comprehend how he could be her husband, therefore he said, "Are Mr. and Mrs. Streetland in?"

"I'm Jake Streetland. Maggie's out. Whatta yuh want?"

It couldn't be that Maggie would leave her son at a time like this and go gossiping as usual, he thought, but that was just what she had done. Jake, as usual, was inebriated, his hair was disheveled, and he stood in his stocking feet without a shirt, wearing only his heavy underwear, trousers and sox. Rex was amused, but the gravity of the situation caused him to refrain from smiling.

"We came to talk with Sonny. Is he in?"

"You leave Sonny alone," he warned with a snap in his voice.

"We didn't come to scold him, Jake," Frank Bosworth said. "We just want to forgive him for Danny's sake; we know he didn't mean to do it."

Jake looked at them dubiously, and evidently he was convinced as to their sincerity, for finally he said gruffly, "Come on in."

As soon as they entered the living room, Rex heard Sonny sobbing in the adjoining bedroom.

"Shut up!" Jake ordered gruffly. "I told you I'd give you another licking if I heard anymore outa yuh, and I meant it."

Rex frowned. He walked softly to the door and opened it slowly. There was Sonny, head buried beneath a pillow sobbing spasmodically.

Rex touched his shoulder and said, "Sonny, this is Reverend Brantford; I came to talk with you."

"Leave me alone," the boy snarled and jerked himself away. "My Mom's told me all about you."

"Sonny, I've come to help you, not harm you."

"Go away. I don't want to talk to you."

"Sonny, Danny's parents are here and they wish to see you."

Sonny threw the pillow aside and jumped up from the bed. "I didn't do nothing. They can't blame me. I didn't do it," he half cried and half screamed. He was trembling and frightened and started to bolt away, but Rex held his shoulder firmly.

"Sonny, nobody's blaming you. We came to tell you Danny forgave you, and his parents came at his request to tell you everything's all right."

"You mean they really ain't mad at me?"

"Of course not. They're in the living room with your dad and want to see you."

"You're sure they ain't going to hurt me?"

"No, Sonny, they're Christians and don't carry grudges. Just before Danny died . . ."

"Did he die? Please, tell me he didn't die. I wanted him to get well; he's my pal."

"I'm sorry," Rex sympathized.

Sonny burst into sobs. Rex folded him in his arms. "You mustn't blame yourself, Sonny, you couldn't help it." He drew his handkerchief and wiped the tears from the lad's eyes. "Now, do you feel like talking with Danny's parents?"

Sonny walked with Rex to the door, still sobbing.

"Don't cry," Mrs. Bosworth comforted him. "Danny didn't want you to feel bad. He's in heaven now and we're going to miss him, so I guess, I guess . . . you'll have to take his place and be my boy. Will you come over and see us?"

"You ain't mad? And you ain't going to shoot me?"

Mr. Bosworth stooped and looked into Sonny's face. "Why would we want to harm you, lad? It wouldn't help matters any and it wouldn't bring Danny back again, now would it?"

"No, but I thought you'd be after me to get me."

"Why no, not since Reverend Brantford taught us that Jesus forgave us, and therefore we should forgive one another."

Rex said in a kindly voice, "Did you ask Jesus to forgive you?"

"No," he answered.

"Why don't you? You'll feel a lot better after you do. How about it?"

Tears welled up into the little fellow's eyes as he lifted his face and nodded his assent.

"All right, Sonny, you pray first, then I'll pray."

"I don't know how to pray," the lad said.

"Didn't your mother ever teach you to pray?"

He shook his head.

"Then just repeat these words after me: Dear Jesus."

"Dear Jesus," he repeated.

"Please forgive my sins . . ." and Sonny began to pray his own prayer, telling the Lord all about the accident and how bad he felt. In his childlike way, he poured out his innermost soul unto the Lord.

Kneeling beside him, Rex put his arm about the boy and interceded for him. When he had finished praying, the boy looked up into his face and said, "You ain't a bad man like my Mom said; you're the nicest friend I ever had . . . except Danny."

Jake had been slouched in a big leather chair listening to the whole procedure without comment, but when Sonny said what he did to Rex, he raised an eyebrow in amazement, but settled down again and said nothing. As Rex and the Bosworths went to the door to leave, Jake didn't bother to bid them good-by, but went to the old iron stove, took off the lid, spit in the fire and pushed more wood into it.

After the visitors were gone, he mumbled, "Beats me. I

thought they'd be mad and try to kill Sonny, but instead they come here and try to comfort him. It just ain't human, it ain't. This forgiveness business got's me plumb licked. Maggie's got religion, so she says, but she ain't never acted like that."

CHAPTER 15

AFTER REX HAD LEFT FOR THE HOSPITAL, CHARLENE put one of her aprons on Dick, tying a beautiful bow knot in back. The small apron emphasized Dick's tall, muscular frame.

"You surely would make a nice housewife for someone," she said saucily. Her teasing eyes sparkled with amusement.

"No one else could get away with this," Dick grumbled. "I'm allergic to washing dishes anyway."

"Who said anything about washing dishes? You're going to dry 'em."

"Get out of my way," he said, "I'm going to wash 'em, so scrape 'em and bring 'em to me."

"Oh no you don't! Those are my mom's best dishes, and I'm not going to let you bust them."

Dick grinned. "We may as well find out who's boss around here. Now you get those dishes and bring 'em here."

Charlene finally yielded. Scraping and stacking the dishes, she brought them to Dick.

"It sure is wonderful your mother's getting well," he said. "You must've worried plenty about her."

"To be real honest, I didn't. I had absolute assurance she would recover, because I prayed and asked God to spare her, and He told me she would live."

Dick was stunned. He stopped washing dishes and stared at her. Finally he asked, "Does God always answer your prayers? Does He always say 'yes'?"

"Yes, God always answers my prayers. There's not one single prayer I've ever uttered that God hasn't heard. Not one request has gone unanswered. There've been times when God told me to wait, and times when He said 'no,' but most generally He says 'yes.' He gives me assurance when He says 'yes.' Didn't Jesus promise, 'Whatsoever ye ask in my name, I will do it'?"

"I wish I could pray," Dick confessed, "but I don't know how."

"Dick, you can't pray until you know Him as your personal Saviour. When once you accept Christ as your personal Saviour, you become a member of God's family, for Jesus said, 'As many as received Him, to them gave he the power to become the *sons of God.*' From then on, as one of His children, you can ask what you will and He'll hear your prayers."

"But can't anyone pray?"

"Yes, anyone can pray, for God loves everyone, but an unsaved person can only pray to God as a creature of His creation. The most acceptable prayer a sinner can pray is, 'God be merciful to me a sinner.'"

Dick was silent. Charlene prayed under her breath, "Lord, this is the moment I've been waiting for, so please help me to win Dick to Christ."

Charlene was setting the dinner plates in the cupboard, when she turned to Dick and said, "Why don't you accept Jesus Christ as your personal Saviour?"

"Charlene, for your sake I would accept Christ."

"But you mustn't do it for my sake. You must do it for Jesus' sake, for He's the One who died for you; He's the One who loves you; He's the One who shed His blood for you."

Dick hesitated. "Charlene, I know I should accept Christ, but I just dread to think of going to the same church that Maggie Streetland and Deacon Wadsworth attend. Those hypocrites! There's enough scrapping going on in the outside world without getting into the church and getting mixed up in the fight that's going on inside the Radford Community Church."

"But, Dick, God loves everyone; He even loves Maggie Streetland and Deacon Wadsworth. They aren't perfect, but God loves them anyway."

"Maybe He does, but that doesn't mean I have to. I heard all about what Deacon Wadsworth is doing. They tell me, he called the deacons together the other night without your dad knowing it and said your dad should be forced to apologize to Maggie Streetland for the way he has been treating her. Imagine! Your dad's never done anything against Maggie Streetland, but she's sure been telling some whopping big lies about him. Why, he even criticized your dad's preaching and then quoted the old adage, 'Where there's smoke, there's fire,' so there must be something to what Maggie's saying. I heard about him circulating that petition, too. He wants to get rid of your dad, the most wonderful man in the world. When they start hurting you, your dad, and your mother, who's been lying at the point of death in the hospital, I don't call that Christianity."

"Neither do I, Dick, but God's Word tells us to love our enemies and to do good to those who do evil against us. I'm sure that if the deacon and Maggie were really saved, they wouldn't act the way they do, but it's not for us to judge; we'll have to leave that up to God. Anyway, the majority of the people in the church aren't agreeing with them, and it isn't fair for you to condemn the whole because of those two."

"If they're not Christians, what're they doing in the church?"

"I said it is not for me to judge whether they're Christians, but if they aren't, we must win them to Christ, and if they are, I'm sure the Lord will punish them for the wrong they're doing."

"Charlene, when the church members prove to me that there is something to Christianity, I promise you, I'll accept Christ as my Saviour."

"But Dick, I insist that Christianity doesn't depend upon Maggie Streetland and Deacon Wadsworth, but upon Jesus Christ. There's nothing wrong with Jesus, regardless of what others are. Jesus never fails!"

"I know, but if there were anything to Christianity, Christians would act differently, wouldn't they?"

Just then Rex Brantford stepped in the door.

"Hello, Daddy! I'm so glad you're back. How's Danny?"

"He died. He's with Jesus. He'll be attending Sunday school in heaven next Sunday."

Rex related the whole story, how they had gone to the Streetland home, and how Mr. and Mrs. Bosworth had put their arms around Sonny Streetland and had forgiven him, even asking him to take Danny's place.

"Jake Streetland appeared to be touched. He'd been so unkind and cruel to Sonny, blaming him and whipping him when what the boy really needed was love and forgiveness. When Jake saw us forgive Sonny, it seemed to puzzle him. I have a feeling that this experience may bring Jake to the Lord. I hope so. We must pray for him."

Dick listened intently. "I didn't think the Bosworths could do that," he said.

Rex added, "I'm so glad little Danny was saved. Only a few weeks ago, he came forward, received Christ as his Saviour, and was baptized. It's wonderful to know he's with the Lord Jesus. Just before he died, he told me to tell Sonny not to feel bad, because he'd be with Jesus in heaven. Danny's father said, 'If this had happened a year ago, I'd have shot Sonny, but now I want to forgive him for Jesus' sake.' In spite of all the troubles, sorrows, and heartaches we have had since we came to pastor this church, it's worthwhile now. When a minister experiences the sorrows and passions of the people back here in the hills as I have tonight and finds that the Gospel of Christ has alleviated the heartache and pain, teaching people to forgive, then any sacrifice, any price to be paid, is worthwhile."

Dick Holland appeared to be deeply touched. He did not stay long after Rex came home. "Thanks again for the wonderful dinner, Charlene," he said. "Thank you, Reverend Brantford, for being so kind to me. I'll have to be going now. My folks'll be wondering what's happened to me if I don't show up soon."

Rex and Charlene stood on the porch and watched him as he walked down the road.

Charlene told her dad about her conversation with Dick. Then the two of them knelt and prayed for him.

As Dick walked down the road, he looked up at the clear sky above. The sun was setting and the evening star already twinkled in the west. Fleecy clouds drifted quickly by. Soon the moon would plate the mountainside with a silver sheen, transforming it into a fairyland. He repeated to himself over and over again the words of Rex Brantford, "I thank God that Danny was saved. If this had happened a year ago, he would've been lost."

"What if that had been me?" Dick wondered. "I'd be lost. One never knows, and it's really dangerous to put off accepting Christ as my Saviour. I should accept Him now."

But the specters of Maggie Streetland and Deacon Wadsworth arose before him, and he murmured, "I surely don't want to get mixed up with those hypocrites."

CHAPTER 16

WITHIN ANOTHER WEEK, THE RADFORD COMMUNITY Church was in a turmoil. The seeds of discontent that had been sown by Maggie Streetland had sprung up and grown as tall as sunflowers in the late summer. A spirit of division had developed within the church, causing people to take sides, one against the other, until lack of trust was in evidence; therefore, the minds of people were completely diverted from winning souls to Christ. Their chief interest was centered upon the quarrel.

Rex Brantford was finding it almost impossible to preach, because there was a spirit of antagonism that quenched the Holy Spirit, and, as a result, his heart was crushed and broken. All of this quarreling and criticism was so contrary to the true teaching of Christ. No matter what he said from the pulpit, someone took offense at his message, whereupon they would go out of the door and immediately say the pastor had criticized them, just to get even with them. As the leader and pastor of the church, he became the target for all of the bickering and backbiting.

Rex spent hours on his knees praying to God, asking the Lord to send a revival into their midst. As one who was wholly and completely yielded to Christ, his heart was filled and overflowing with love. The people were even quarreling over him, some fighting for him, and some fighting against him. Nevertheless, they were fighting, and even though the majority were on Rex's side, he couldn't be happy over the spirit of division and strife. He wanted to leave and withdraw himself, rather than to become the focal point of a quarrel.

At times he thought, *If I am the source of the trouble, I should go.* But then he recognized that really he was not the source of the trouble, and regardless who the pastor might be, he would face the same problems and difficulties. The people needed to get their hearts right with God.

Rex began to preach plain sermons on the subjects of forgiveness, Christian love, and the indwelling of the Holy Spirit, but his sermons went forth as a cry into a chasm with an empty echo. His efforts were seemingly a waste of time.

Inasmuch as Deacon Wadsworth had discovered that his petition to get rid of the pastor had met with a rebuff and had boomeranged on him, he concluded something had to be done to save his own reputation. Assuming the difficulty to be that the people were not psychologically prepared as yet, he proceeded to properly condition their minds for the coming annual business meeting by calling a secret meeting of the board of deacons without the knowledge or consent of the pastor. The first Rex knew of this meeting was when the telephone rang, and Deacon Wadsworth said, "Reverend Brantford, we're in a deacons' meeting and it's urgent that you come at once. We would like for you to appear before the board to answer some very vital questions."

For a moment Rex was stunned. "Who called the meeting?" he asked. "You had no authority to do so." At first he thought he should refuse to come, but after consideration, he decided it would be wisdom to acquiesce and accede to their request.

"I'll be right over," he said. "Where are you meeting? At the church?"

"Yes, at the church. We'll be waiting for you."

When Rex Brantford walked into the meeting, most of the deacons were embarrassed. It was evident they were being misguided by Deacon Wadsworth into becoming tools for his scheme.

There stood Deacon Wadsworth in his customary threadbare, gray-black, one and only suit. His light gray vest sported a big watch chain. His wizened, sallow face was wrinkled with deep furrows. His pinched nose was partly hidden with nose glasses. The wrinkles on his face moved as he opened and closed his mouth, tasting his own satisfying words, while his beady eyes danced with serpentine satisfaction. He was a tall, lanky, unscrupulous politician.

However, Deacon Wadsworth was too clever to be the spokesman, so with a sour apologetic grin, he said, "The deacons have some questions they'd like to ask you if you'd be so kind as to answer them."

"I'll do the best I can, brethren, so go ahead and ask me whatever you will," Rex replied.

One of the deacons, who was easily influenced and led in any direction, asked the first question. "Reverend Brantford, we deacons feel that you spent entirely too much time visiting with your wife in the hospital. You neglected your visitation of the membership and other church work."

This criticism struck fire in Rex Brantford's heart. Was it possible that people who called themselves Christians could be cruel enough to criticize him for visiting his wife when she was hovering between life and death? He felt his anger rising, but he remembered the Scriptural command, "The servant of God must not strive."

Rex answered quietly, "Will you be more specific? In what way have I neglected any member of our church or any church activity?"

There was complete silence.

Rex had been working night and day until he was exhausted. With his wife in the hospital, he had still continued to faithfully serve them, even though they had greatly added many burdens upon his shoulders by telephoning criticisms, gossip, and morsels of slander. Always they phoned him on the basis of friendship, because they felt he should know about a particular matter. Nevertheless, these calls had occupied many precious hours of his time.

"Is it true, Reverend Brantford, that you have received money from the relief fund of the church to assist you in paying your hospital bills?" another deacon queried.

Rex's face turned scarlet. He ground his teeth and clenched his fists. This was almost more than he could bear, for he had not received any assistance from anyone. Instead, he had prayed night and day for divine assistance, wondering how he would be able to meet the hospital expense, but no one in the church had come to his rescue. *It's mighty small,* he thought to himself, *that anyone would be critical if such assistance had been given.* For a moment he almost exploded and told them what he thought of their pettiness and lack of love. Then, as a servant of the Lord and as a faithful minister of the Gospel, he quietly replied, "That isn't true."

"I think that we should call a special business meeting of the church so Mrs. Streetland may bring her accusations against our pastor," Deacon Wadsworth proposed. "I think he should be forced to face her and answer her charges. Don't you agree, brethren?"

Only one deacon agreed. "Yes, the Bible states that if you have ought against a person you should go to them, therefore this matter should be dealt with publicly."

Rex Brantford stood to his feet. He was disappointed and his countenance was sad.

"Brethren," he began, "my heart's burdened for Mrs. Street-land. I assure you I have never done anything against her, but on the contrary, I have sacrificially aided her son when he was in serious difficulty. It is my prayer that somehow we will be able to demonstrate the true meaning of Christian love and forgive-ness to Mrs. Streetland. In so doing, I pray that, by example, I may be able to teach her the Christian life in all its beauty. If such a meeting as you suggest were called, bitterness would result and it would make it impossible for me ever to win Mrs. Streetland, and the church would be hopelessly torn and split beyond repair. Your pastor would be humiliated to such an extent his usefulness in this community would cease. Very likely he would be compelled to resign this pulpit."

The mere suggestion of the pastor's resignation pleased Deacon

Wadsworth so much, he was unable to hide the grin that spread over his thin lips.

Some of the deacons insisted on a meeting of the pastor with Mrs. Streetland, but Rex was adamant and would not yield. "I'll not attend such a meeting even if it's arranged," he said. "I'll resign my pulpit before I'll yield."

On the other hand, Rex was a kind, loving pastor. He tactfully avoided quarreling with these men by assuring them, "I love you all and pray for you daily. There's no reason why we shouldn't work together for the glory of Christ."

"We feel you've been away in meetings too often," another deacon insisted.

"I must admit that from the human viewpoint, it may have been premature for me to leave you and go away for a meeting as soon as I did; however, when I came you agreed that I would be free to conduct evangelistic meetings on the outside as God granted opportunity if I felt led of the Lord to go. In the future, we'll discuss these matters with you prayerfully, but I warn you, I must obey the voice of God. I don't think the work has suffered during the few days I was absent."

The most aggravating criticism of the evening was that his sermons were too long, for, after all, he had only been preaching short messages of thirty to thirty-five minutes. *It is evident,* he thought, *the difficulty is their own lack of spirituality. They are not interested in winning souls to Christ, nor in learning the Word of God, for they don't hunger and thirst after righteousness. They're "playing church."*

They criticized the type of messages, and even his delivery, but Rex was big enough to thank them for their criticisms. He then asked them for their prayers. He recognized that all of these matters would clear up when once they made right their hearts with the Lord. *It is my task and duty as a pastor to love them, win them, lead them, and direct them into the deeper spiritual life which is made possible by complete yieldedness to God and the infilling of the Holy Spirit.*

"Now if you'll excuse me, gentlemen, I must leave and go to the hospital. Mrs. Jones underwent a serious emergency operation this afternoon. She needs her pastor, so shall we have a word of prayer before I leave?" Immediately, Rex led in prayer, not awaiting their approval.

While enroute to the hospital, Rex gave serious thought to the nominating committee for the annual business meeting. He didn't know whom he could trust for that committee, because not many would have the wisdom to deal with this serious situation, and some of these deacons weren't spiritually fit to fill the office of deacon. Of course, the answer to all of the problems was a great spiritual awakening, a revival, so he prayed that God would pour out the Holy Spirit in their midst and send a revival. "Oh God, give me courage and strength to fight this battle through to the end. Lord, I'll not leave and run from this task as would a coward, but please give me wisdom, Lord."

Back at the church, some of the deacons continued to cauterize the pastor until one o'clock in the morning, but finally, one by one, they departed and went home.

Rex refused to tell Blanche what had occurred at the deacons' meeting. Nevertheless, she knew he was troubled about something for he couldn't sleep that night. About three o'clock in the morning, he arose and spent the rest of the night on his knees in prayer. One thing was certain: he couldn't tell her what had happened.

All that night, Rex wondered how the situation would end. He could see no way out. One thing definitely encouraged him; the majority of the deacons had remained silent throughout the meeting, and it was evident that their sympathies were with him. They seemed to understand. "More important than that," he repeated to himself, " 'If God be for us, who can be against us?' I have a great God. There is no problem too great for Him, and though I can't cope with the situation, somehow God will solve my problem. There are no blind alleys or dead-end streets when we follow Him."

CHAPTER 17

THE WIND HAD BEEN WHISTLING THROUGH THE EAVES of the house throughout the night, blowing bitter cold weather. A powdery snow had whitened the hillsides and topped the evergreens like frosting on a cake. The hemlocks seemed to mourn as the wind whined through their needles. The full moon transformed the wilds into an enchanted paradise whenever it peeked through the snow clouds, but it had disappeared by the time Rex arose and went to the kitchen to start a fire in the cooking stove. Soon the kettle was humming a comforting tune, so Rex went to the back porch and looked at the thermometer.

"Ten below!" he whistled. Shivering, he hurried back to the warmth of the stove.

The night before, ten friends, men from his former parish, had arrived as his guests for the opening day of deer season. Inasmuch as there was not enough room to entertain them in the one extra bedroom, cots were set up in the living room and attic.

Ere long, the aroma of coffee and frying bacon penetrated the entire house awakening everyone, but the men in the attic found it difficult to forsake the warmth of their beds to brave the cold. The fragrance of pancakes furnished the added zest necessary to arouse them to dress and hurry down stairs, carrying their boots with them.

Once down stairs, a cheerful fire crackled in the open fireplace of the living room, so they sat near enough to feel its warmth as they laced their boots. The conversation centered upon former hunting experiences, some of them too bizarre to be taken seriously. Laughter rang through the house until happiness became contagious.

Blanche, though still extremely weak, had insisted on Rex inviting his friends and had promised she would not assume any responsibilities in entertainment, but now, even she couldn't resist the urge to join the enthusiastic hunters who sat about the table devouring pancakes with insatiable appetites which the mountain air seemed to create. When she entered the living room, she was welcomed with enthusiasm, and also with some apologies for having awakened her.

"You didn't awaken me," she said, "it was the aroma of coffee, bacon and pancakes . . . plus all the fun. This is like a tonic to me. May I have some cakes, too, Rex?"

"Coming up!" he answered.

A voice from upstairs called, "Daddy, may I come down? It smells so good, and I'm hungry."

"Come ahead! I'll pour your coffee and the cakes are already cooked."

"Rex, aren't you going to eat?" Blanche asked. "Let me cook some cakes for you."

"Uh, uh! You agreed you wouldn't do any work while the men were here. Remember? A bargain's a bargain, and, besides, I'll have plenty to eat when I've finished filling up all these silos. More coming up, fellows," he said as he shoved another platter of pancakes onto the table.

After cooking all the cakes the men could eat, Rex said, "I've just got to get a breath of air," and he went to the front door and stepped outside. He wasn't actually interested in fresh air; he was impatient for the dawn and wishfully searched the sky in a fruit-less search for the first streaks of light in the eastern sky, but in-stead, the morning star was shining like a distant torch and the darkest hour of the night had settled over the earth. His curiosity overcame him, so he took his flashlight and shone it into the forest to see if any deer were there. Two silvery green eyes reflected in the light, and a smile of hope broke upon his face.

"I wonder if that's Old Skeleton?" he murmured. "Everyone wants to get rid of him, but I hope he makes it through this year; he deserves to live, the smart old codger. He'd be too tough to eat, anyhow."

"B-r-r-r, it's cold," he shivered and ran back into the house.

The night before, Rex and his entire group of friends had met at the house of Frank Bettor to lay plans for the day's hunt. Frank had been born and raised in these hills, and his grandfather, John, had been the first settler in that area. When John had first moved into the mountains, the only other residents were Indians, who taught him every hunting and fishing trick they knew, and they also shared with him their knowledge of the secret game trails and the habits of the deer. He had been killed at Gettysburg, dur-ing the Civil War, leaving Frank's father to shift for himself in the same mountains. In turn, his father taught Frank the secrets the Indians taught him.

Frank was a medium sized man with a philosophical, thin face, and squeegee eyelids that blinked nervously like moving windshield wipers. He was uneducated, though he could read to a limited extent. His optimistic outlook on life was based on an original, sensible viewpoint. He always dressed in work clothes and wore a hunting cap summer and winter.

He was a dead shot with a rifle; therefore, he had been ex-cluded from all turkey shoots, because no one else would enter the contest if he were shooting in competition with them.

All of the natives of the hills were Annie Oakleys with deer rifles. One of the natives who had planned to hunt with Rex's party was a full-blooded Iroquois Indian, who would shoot beneath a tin can, fifty yards distance, spin it up into the air, and then put a bullet through the middle of it while it was in mid-air.

One of the young men of the mountains never carried a rifle, only a revolver. When Rex asked him to demonstrate his shoot-ing ability, he said, "Do you see that snow bird on that twig?"

"Yes, are you going to hit it with that revolver?"

"No, I'm going to shoot the twig from beneath his feet."

He did and the bird flew away.

Most of the natives who had asked to hunt with Rex were not Christians, but he invited them to join the party; he was hoping to win them to Christ. The first time they met, Frank extended his hand in friendship but limited its significance by saying, "Preacher, I'll be glad to hunt with you, but I want you to get one thing straight: if I want to cuss, I'll cuss, and when I want to swear, I'll swear, and if I want to tell a dirty story, I'll tell a dirty story."

Rex smiled and replied, "Frank, if I want to pray, I'll pray, and if I want to preach, I'll preach, and if I want to talk to you about Jesus, I'll talk to you about Jesus."

After that, Frank never cussed, swore, nor told a dirty story in the presence of the preacher, but the preacher kept his end of the bargain and gave Frank a Bible. Each night during hunting season, Rex made a habit of inviting the boys to come to the parsonage for Bible reading and prayer. At first they resented it and refused, but, eventually they came and enjoyed it, until finally it was Frank who asked, "Come on, Preacher. When're you gonna tell us more about that Book and Jesus?"

The night before the big hunt, they spent most of their time trying to figure out how they could outwit Old Skeleton.

Old Skeleton had a habit of lying up on the top edge of a steep, unscalable mountainside, where wheat fields flanked him, making it impossible for a hunter to approach without being detected. He would watch the valley below and observe the hunters as they took their stations; then when the drivers would come through, he would sneak in between the watchers and escape without being seen. Repeatedly, this had happened. If Old Skeleton were pressed too hard, he would sneak across the road and run into the slashings along the creek bed near Jake Streetland's place where, he seemed to know, no one dared to hunt.

Frank said, "We're going to fool Old Skeleton this time by doing the craziest thing any hunters have ever done. Before daybreak, Preacher, I want you and four fellows to walk up the old Dug Road between the two mountains and hide in the slashings. Watch the opposite hillside. Four of us will walk four miles down the main road to where the mountain begins, at Laurel Point, and we'll beat the brush all the way around the mountain. Just as soon as we come to the opposite side of the Dug Road, I want three fellows to come through the wheat fields toward the steep mountainside as fast as they can run, making all the noise they can. Old Skeleton will be hiding up there, and he'll be so confused he won't know which way to turn."

Naturally, the conversation at the breakfast table centered around Old Skeleton. When breakfast was finished, the men put on their brilliant red and black coats, took their rifles, and departed to their assigned stations.

"Do be careful," Blanche warned as she kissed Rex good-by.

"Don't worry," he replied. "You're the one who must be careful."

"Oh, I'll be all right; I'm almost well, you know, so you just go out and have a good time. Be sure to bring back Old Skeleton. We'll clean off the dining room table so you can skin him right here tonight."

"That's a promise! We'll do it."

A certain amount of mumbling and whispering was unavoidable, but the boys had agreed to walk silently to their posts. Halfway up the Dug Road, Rex took his station and watched the mountainside expectantly. Deer had a way of appearing and disappearing just like ghosts.

In the east, the first streaks of red and yellow were beginning to pierce the blue and purple sky. It was time for the drive to start. Soon, Frank and the boys would be beating the brush, swishing whips through the air and hitting the brush. That seemed to frighten the deer more than anything.

Suddenly, Rex heard a limb break and a crashing of timber on the mountainside. The sound drew nearer and nearer. Expectantly, almost breathlessly, he moved the safety on his rifle to off and raised his gun to his shoulder. He could now see the branches of small trees along the mountainside moving. *It must be a buck*, he thought. *Doe don't travel like that.*

Then, suddenly, the deer came into sight, just for a moment. His rack was laid back up on his shoulders, proving he was an old buck. The deer stopped and stood still when he came to the bank of a stream. Rex knew that within a split second the deer would leap across the creek and quickly disappear, so he squeezed the trigger. The cracking sound of the rifle reverberated through the mountains, breaking the sacred stillness, and the deer leaped twenty feet over the stream and ran down into the valley, in strides of twenty to thirty feet. Rex fired another shot, but missed.

He caught a fleeting glimpse of the buck's white tail; then, the tail dropped, indicating the deer was wounded.

Rex called to the other watchers. "I'm going after him, so don't shoot me by mistake." Running down the valley, he came to a gulley, and there he saw the deer lying on his back with his feet in the air. After examining the deer carefully, he was thrilled to discover he had made a perfect shot, hitting him below the shoulder and through the heart. Excitedly, he turned the deer over and proceeded to tag and dress him.

Taking a long rope from the back pocket of his coat, Rex tied it around the horns of the deer and dragged him to the Indian's cabin. After hanging him on an apple tree, he stood and admired his trophy. "He's a beauty! Eight points," he bragged.

There were two other deer shot during that drive, but not Old Skeleton. Yes, he had come down off the mountainside. They found his great broad tracks which could belong to only one deer in the mountains, for they were the biggest buck tracks anyone had ever seen.

The tracks indicated there were three doe with Old Skeleton, for the toe of their tracks came to a point, and were shaped more like a heart. Once again, Old Skeleton had outwitted the hunters, this time, by walking a few feet behind one of the hunters who never even heard or saw him, because his three doe had deliberately attracted his attention by walking in front of him in plain view.

One of the men admitted, "I saw Old Skeleton and could've shot him."

"Well, why under the sun didn't you?" Frank bellowed.

"Because, Frank, he was stalking just a few feet behind you, and when you'd take a few steps, he'd follow you, and when you stopped, he stopped. He stuck so close to you, I didn't dare to shoot, because I was afraid the bullet might ricochet and hit you. He's a smart old buck."

"I don't believe it!" Frank said. "What's more, I'll prove it ain't so."

He walked back up the mountainside, and sure enough there were the deer tracks to prove that Old Skeleton had followed him around the mountainside. He returned with a sheepish grin and began to laugh. "We'll get him yet. Tomorrow maybe. But right now, fellows, don't you think we ought to see what these sandwiches taste like?"

The men reached into the back of their coats and quickly pulled out their thermos bottles of coffee and their sandwiches.

Sitting down on the cold rocks, they talked about the tricks Old Skeleton had performed during the past twenty years. Then Frank told them about the game warden coming up there the past summer and catching a bear. "The bear got away from him and climbed up a tree, so he had to cut the tree down to get the bear," he said.

"By the way," one of the hunters said, "you may not have known it, but you put two black bear up on that drive you just made. They came by me like bullets and looked like balls of fur rolling along the ground at about ninety miles an hour, I'd say. The little trees in front of 'em didn't bother them one bit. They just knocked 'em out of the way and kept going. I yelled at them, but they didn't pay any attention. One would've run smack over me if I hadn't stepped aside real quick. Sure mighty lucky for those bear the season for them closed last week, otherwise I'd have me a bear for sure."

"Pshaw," another hunter said. "You know good and well you couldn't hit them ba'r. You was so scared you couldn't even have pulled that trigger, and if you had, you would of hit most anything but those ba'r."

The fellow on the further end of the watch said, "The doe you scared up on that drive were as thick as sheep; in fact, there were so many of 'em, they were jumping over each other. Then, all of a sudden, they broke and whipped over the mountaintop."

"Well, let 'em keep on running," Frank answered. "What do you say we go back to the preacher's house, get into our cars, and drive down the road to the John Canyon? There ought to be a lot of deer in there."

CHAPTER 18

As THE BAND OF HUNTERS CAME DOWN TO THE ROAD-way, their eyes automatically scanned the mountainside on the other side of the valley beyond the creek. It was just as steep as a cliff, and few men could boast that they had ever scaled it, for though it appeared to be bare rock, it wasn't. It was filled with holes, gullies, and crevices, where much vegetation grew and deer could safely graze without danger of interference. When deer were hunted hard, they invariably fled to this refuge, and at times they could be seen grazing there like so many cattle or sheep.

One of the hunters, Slim, had eyes like an eagle, and would

spot deer when an untrained eye couldn't see them. Because Slim
was a natural born woodsman, the slightest motion on the hillside
would attract his attention.

Suddenly Slim cried, "Hey look! There are four deer! I believe the leader of the group is a buck. Give me your glasses
quick, George!"

George fumbled in the case, pulled out his highpowered glasses,
and handed them to Slim. "That's a buck, all right! He holds his
head back, hiding his horns on his shoulders so they won't get
caught as he runs through the bramble. They see us. See them
running? The buck's in the lead. Don't hit the other three.
They're doe."

Immediately, the hunters began to shoot, and it sounded
like the Second World War had just begun again. A tremendous
amount of lead was pouring into the hillside, and the din of rifles
cracking was deafening.

Rex did not so much as raise his gun, and for more than one
reason he stepped aside from the group. In the first place, he had
already shot his deer. In addition to that, he realized it was not
legal to shoot from a roadway, and though they were far back in
the mountains, and no one would probably ever know that they
were shooting from the highway, it was still illegal, and Rex obeyed
the law implicitly.

One of the main reasons Rex did not join in the shooting was
the danger that, during the excitement, someone was apt to be
hurt by stepping in front of the line of fire of another hunter.

Round after round of shot was fired into the hillside while
Slim watched through the glasses. "You got him! You got him!"
Slim cried. "The buck is down! Those two pulling ahead of him
are doe. Don't shoot them. Keep on shooting! He's wounded but
he got up and is running again. There, that shot got him! He's
down. Let's go get him."

In their excitement, none of the group had stopped to consider that they were shooting directly over Jake Streetland's farm
until they heard the door slam and saw Jake come out, dressed in
his customary red and black checkered shirt. As usual, he was
drunk. Shaking his fist, he cried, "Preacher Brantford, this is your
doings. You know better than to allow that gang of yours to
shoot across my farm and scare my sheep to death. I'm going to
get my shot gun and blow your head off!"

Jake put his hand on the doorknob to go inside, but the moment he did so, there was a hurried clattering of steel as every

man in the group threw a fresh shell into the chamber of his gun, cocked it, and raised the gun ready to fire. It was Frank who cried at the top of his voice, "Jake, if you take one step, you're a dead man! Don't move! Stand right where you are!"

The men all knew Jake Streetland. They knew that he was drunk enough to carry out his threat, and it would be too late to stop him after he had his gun. He would kill the preacher.

Rex's heart beat fast and he became as pale as death. He didn't tremble at the thought of dying, but he did fear that a murder was about to take place in which he would be involved, a murder for which he was not responsible. He had often prayed for Jake, and he wanted him to be saved, not slain. *How slick the devil is*, Rex thought.

Jake didn't move, for, drunk as he was, he knew one step meant certain death. Frank walked to the door and shoved Jake aside. Disregarding the remonstrance of Maggie Streetland, who had come to the door, he took Jake's gun from the gun rack, unloaded it, and brought it outside.

The men lowered their guns and Frank said, "You can go in now, Jake."

Jake fumbled with the door knob and finally opened the door. Standing upon the threshold, he shook his fist at Rex Brantford, and threatened, "Preacher, I'll kill you yet. I'll getcha. Mind what I say. I'll getcha. And there won't be no gang around to help you when I do." And with that he went inside and slammed the door.

"Phew! Boy, and he means it," the fellows said one to another.

While a couple of the boys stood on the road to see to it that Jake Streetland didn't cause any more trouble, the rest of them crossed his farm, climbed the mountainside and retrieved the deer. He was a beautiful buck.

They encountered no difficulty in bringing the deer down the mountain, for it was so steep, they had all they could do to keep him from falling from cliff to cliff. Once they had brought him to the valley, they cleaned him, roped his horns, and dragged him along the creek until they reached Brantford's house, where they hung him on an apple tree.

As they were walking along the creek, near the edge of Streetland farm, Rex noticed something reflecting in the sunlight. It was partly buried in the snow, so out of curiosity he stooped to pick it up. To his amazement, it was a large switchblade knife with a yellow handle. *Someone must've lost it,* he thought. He put it in his pocket.

With a panel truck, the boys went over to the Indian's hut and brought back the other deer. They strung the two deer side by side in Rex's back yard.

The fellows stood around and proudly admired their kill as they planned for the next day's hunt.

Both Blanche and Charlene were thrilled when they looked outside and saw the deer.

When once inside the house, they threw off their heavy coats and wearily sank down into the chairs in front of the warm fireplace. They chatted about the happenings of the day, all of them, of course, carefully avoiding discussing the excitement of the afternoon. No one mentioned Jake Streetland's threat.

"Oh yes," Rex said as he felt the uncomfortable switchblade knife in his pocket, "I found this knife half buried beneath the snow." He laid it on the table.

"Dick, would you have any idea whose knife it is?"

"Dick, isn't that the same knife Gary Streetland drew on you the night of the hayride?" Charlene asked.

"Looks like it. Let me see it." Dick studied the yellow handle. "It's the same color."

Rex questioned, "How do you open the blade on that knife?"

"Here. Just like this," Dick replied. The blade sprang out. It was stained with blood!

Rex frowned. He purposely didn't mention that he had found it on the Streetland farm. He pushed the blade back and held the knife in his hand, wondering just what he should do.

"What's the matter, Rex?" Blanche asked. "What're you thinking about?"

"Oh, nothing." He quickly returned the knife to his pocket.

As soon as the evening meal was finished, Rex excused himself without explanation and left the house. When Blanche heard him start the car, she said, "I wonder what's on his mind? Something's bothering him."

Blanche's remark brought a momentary pause in the conversation of the guests, but almost immediately their chatter resumed and became more hilarious than before as they reviewed the hunt of the day.

Rex drove to the state police headquarters where he found Sergeant Wellington on duty at the desk.

"Good evening, Preacher. What can we do for you?" the sergeant asked.

"Sergeant, I was hunting today and found this switchblade knife near the creek, back of the Streetland homestead."

The sergeant took the knife and released the blade. "Whew!" he whistled. "That's blood on the blade, and handle, too. This could be the weapon used in the attack on your wife!"

"Exactly! That's what I thought."

"Thank you, Reverend. A test in the laboratory will reveal whether that is human blood, and we'll find out immediately." He pressed the button on his desk and his assistant came. "Here, take this to the laboratory immediately, and have them run a test on the blood on the blade and handle of this knife to see if it's human blood. We'll want to know the blood type, of course, and other routine information."

"That knife," Rex said, "looks exactly like the knife Gary Streetland has been known to carry."

"That's worth knowing," Sergeant Wellington said. "This may be the lead we've been looking for, and if it is stained with human blood, we'll investigate to discover whether Gary is the owner. That shouldn't be too difficult to determine. Thank you, sir."

"You're very welcome. By the way, please let me know as to the outcome of your investigations; I'll be anxious to know, but please don't inform my wife, because it would be better not to revive her memories of her experience. She's still quite weak."

Rex returned home without his guests even having missed him, but Blanche asked, "Where have you been?"

"Getting some fresh air," he answered.

"Fresh air! Oh, well. If you don't want to tell me, you don't have to."

Rex was so weary from the day's hunt, he slept well that night despite his worries, and the next morning he was awake before daybreak, cooking pancakes and sausage for his guests who proved a little harder to arouse than the morning before. Hunting was good that day, so much so, they had their camp limit of deer by noon, a total of six deer in all, so they cleaned their deer, divided the meat, and departed for home.

"It was all too short a time," Rex complained, "but I'm glad they got the limit."

CHAPTER 19

MAGGIE STREETLAND WAS LAZILY PUTTING AWAY THE supper dishes when there was a knock on the door. She breathed heavily as she stopped to wipe the perspiration from her forehead with her apron.

As usual, Jake was sitting in front of the old iron stove in the living room in his stocking feet, reading the newspaper. He was in a stupor of drunkenness to the extent that he was somewhat subdued for a change. In fact, he had just dozed off to sleep when the sharp knock was heard throughout the house. At first, Jake didn't hear it. But the knock grew louder and louder. Jake awakened enough to shout to his wife, "Hey Maw, somebody's at the front door. You'd better answer it."

"You good-for-nothing, lazy bum! Why don't you get up and answer it yourself?"

Jake was undisturbed. He knew his wife would answer it. She just had to fuss a little bit to make herself feel better. He had become accustomed to her nagging and growling. He readjusted his glasses and started to look for the place he had lost in the article he was reading in the newspaper.

As Maggie opened the door, she suddenly became speechless, a rare event for her. She swallowed, put on her best front, and said, "C-c-come in."

Two state policemen asked as they entered, "This is the Streetland residence, I believe?"

"Wh . . . why, yes."

Jake leaned forward in his chair and expended enough energy to look around. He suddenly came to life and jumped to his feet. "Whatcha want here anyway?"

"Is your son, Gary, home? We'd like to talk with him."

"Gary?" Maggie asked. "Gary? He's done nothing. What do you want with my son? He's a good boy. He's always good to his mother, never runs around, never does anything really bad. Oh, of course, sometimes he gets himself into little scrapes, but they don't amount to anything."

"We only wish to ask him some questions, Ma'am."

"You can't have him. I won't let you take my boy. You just

want him so you can frame him for something. You can't come into our house like this."

"Lady, take your choice. Either your son will come with us willingly, or otherwise, we'll return with a search warrant and force him to go."

Maggie immediately went into one of her hysterical spells and began to scream and cry.

Jake, drunk as he was, realized Maggie was only making matters worse, slowly arose from his chair and mumbled to Maggie as he went to the dining room, " 'Tain't no use, Maw. If the law wants him, they'll get him, and you can't stop 'em. If Gary ain't done nothin', there ain't no use worrying."

Opening the door to the stairs he called gruffly, "Hey, Gary, come on down here! Some cops wanta talk with you."

Gary, having already heard the commotion, had been eavesdropping. His chin quivered; his face paled; he trembled with fear. He tried to call back, but couldn't talk. His palpitating heart beat fast, and every muscle in his cheek jerked spasmodically.

Gary had been acting strangely, was grouchy and easily upset, so his parents couldn't even talk to him. Whenever questioned by them, he went into a frenzy and retired upstairs to his room. He spent most of his time alone. Therefore, his parents sensed that something was wrong. Just what, they didn't know.

"Gary!" Jake yelled again. " 'Tain't no use trying to run away. Come on down here."

Gary looked at the window. He thought of jumping and trying to escape, but after consideration concluded, "Might get shot if I try that."

Slowly he came downstairs, step by step, but his mind was churning like a windmill. *What will I say?* he wondered, but there was no time to think about that now. *I never thought that they'd ever guess it was me. Who told 'em anyway? How'd they find out I did it? Do they really know, or are they just guessing?* As Gary stepped into the living room, one of the policemen slapped handcuffs on him.

Maggie screamed, "You're treating him as if he were a criminal. What's he supposed to have done anyway?"

"It's pretty serious, Ma'am. They want him at headquarters to question him regarding attempted murder."

"No, no!" Maggie cried.

Gary, in a daze, walked out of the door between the two policemen.

As the car pulled away, Jake said, "Now, Maw, there's no sense getting excited over nothing."

"Over nothing? What're you talking about? They're going to electrocute Gary."

"Now Maw, they can't burn Gary unless he's done something, and if he has, there ain't nothin' we can do about it."

"It's that preacher, that Rex Brantford! He's gone and accused our boy of committing a murder. I always said he'd do something to get even with us."

Maggie went to the telephone, and said, "Operator, give me 22-516, ring three."

On the other end of the line, Deacon Wadsworth answered, "Hello." By this time Maggie was shouting at the top of her voice.

"Now Maggie, wait a minute! Wait a minute! Say that all over again, will you? I didn't get it. You say that Reverend Brantford has had Gary arrested? For what? What did the boy do? What did he accuse him of? Murder? My land, no! He couldn't accuse Gary of murder unless he murdered someone. Who did he murder?"

"I don't know," Maggie replied, "but the state police came and arrested him and took him to jail. There's only one person who would accuse him of murder, and it's that awful preacher."

Before Maggie hung up, every one on the party line knew what had happened and the story soon spread through the valley that Gary had committed a murder. Some thought Maggie said, "Rex Brantford murdered Gary."

"No, you're wrong," others said. "Gary murdered Rex Brantford and is in jail, waiting to be electrocuted tomorrow morning."

As soon as Jake, who was now sobered considerably, was able to hush up Maggie and get her off the phone, he rang for Dr. John Holliday. "Better hurry right over," he said. "Maggie's having one of her spells."

Doctor Holliday, upon arriving at the Streetland home, decided that he would have done better to have studied to be a psychiatrist rather than a general practitioner. Maggie Streetland was definitely neurotic to the breaking point, and though he tried to reason with her, it was futile. Finally, he opened up his case, took out the needle, and gave Maggie a shot of nembutal, but even that failed to quiet her down.

At the parsonage, Rex Brantford was just beating Dick Holland in a game of chess when the phone rang. Charlene, who had been washing the dishes in the kitchen, answered the phone and excitedly called, "It's for you, Daddy. Something important evidently."

Pushing his chair back carefully so as not to disturb the chess board, Rex said, "Excuse me, please, Dick. I'll be back in just a minute and we'll finish this game."

"Hello. Reverend Brantford speaking."

"Reverend Brantford," said Mr. Osgood, "something terrible's happened. Gary Streetland has just been arrested by the state police on a charge of murder."

"Murder? Who's been murdered?"

Mr. Osgood answered, "I don't know, Reverend Brantford, but the police came and got him and took him off to jail. Maggie Streetland is beside herself and gone all to pieces. They're saying all up and down the valley you are the one who had him arrested, and I think that's a terrible thing for a preacher to do."

"I? I don't know anything about it."

"Well, that's what they're saying. I don't know just what you can do about it."

"Very well," Rex said, "I'll go right over and see Maggie and try to straighten this thing out."

After the conversation on the phone had ended, Rex said, "Please excuse me, Dick; Charlene will have to finish that game of chess with you. I think I had you beaten, but if she takes over, maybe you can turn the tables and beat her. I must go see Mrs. Streetland; Gary's been arrested!"

"Arrested? What for?" Charlene asked.

"Murder," Rex said.

"But who's been murdered, Daddy?"

Dick Holland sat wide-eyed and with open mouth, listening to the conversation. "Gary? Arrested? That just can't be. And yet, I wouldn't put it past him. His mother's spoiled him to the point where he thinks he can get away with anything because she'll take his side and cover up for him, but this's one time she won't be able to help her little boy, not if it's murder!"

Rex was putting on his hat and coat when Blanche came downstairs. "Rex, what's wrong? Where are you going?"

"To Streetlands. They've just arrested Gary, and Maggie's gone to pieces. I'll be back as soon as I can."

It was only two farms down to Streetlands', so in a matter of minutes, Rex was there. When Rex knocked on the door, he could hear Maggie screaming inside.

"Come on in," Jake said and opened the door.

Rex stepped to the couch where Maggie lay sobbing, Doctor Holliday still by her side. "Mrs. Streetland, I'm so sorry. I'm sure Gary isn't guilty of anything so drastic as murder, so you mustn't worry. Just trust God and let's commit Gary to God in prayer. Shall I lead in prayer?"

"You? You pray about it when you're the one who got Gary into this trouble in the first place? I should say not!"

"Believe me, Mrs. Streetland, I had nothing to do with this. I didn't even know what had happened until a few minutes ago, but I assure you I'll see Gary tomorrow and help him in any way possible. That is, of course, providing he has not already returned home by then."

Rex opened his Testament and proceeded to read the 23rd Psalm, but it was doubtful that Maggie heard what he read.

As Rex left the Streetland house and started homeward, he felt very despondent, for his efforts to comfort seemed so in vain. Maggie wouldn't listen.

Rex Brantford suspected that the arrest had been made on the basis of the evidence of the switchblade knife he had turned over to the police, but as he considered the possibility of Gary committing such a crime, he remarked to himself, "He wouldn't do a thing like that; he wouldn't be capable of such a crime, and why would he ever want to stab Blanche? What have we done against Gary to warrant such an attack upon any member of our family? It just doesn't make sense."

CHAPTER 20

AT STATE POLICE HEADQUARTERS, GARY UNDERWENT a stiff examination. "Where were you the night Mrs. Brantford was attacked?" the officers asked.

"I don't know nothin'. What's more, I ain't gonna talk. I'm not gonna answer no questions."

"If you don't wish to cooperate, we have ways of making you."

"I told you I don't know nothin', and I'm not tellin' you nothin'."

"I repeat, where were you on the night this attack was made?"

"I was up in my bedroom sleeping. My ma and pa will tell you so."

One of the policemen laid the switchblade knife on the table. Gary's eyes widened.

"Where'd you get that?" he asked.

"Is that your knife, Gary?"

"No, that ain't my knife."

"Then how does it happen, if it isn't yours, that your finger-prints were found on it?"

"What if it is my knife? That doesn't prove nothin'."

"Except that it is stained with human blood."

"So what? I cut my finger with it."

"I see. In that case, we'll just take your blood and see if it's the same as the blood on the knife. Incidentally, why did you go to the general store, the day after the crime, and buy another knife?"

"Because I lost my knife. I lost it down by the creek. I'll betcha Dick Holland found it, didn't he? He's always snooping around our farm. He's probably the one who did the stabbing, after he found my knife, and now he's trying to put the blame on me."

"Sorry, that explanation won't hold water, because the knife wasn't found until last week. It was found on your farm right where you threw it."

"Who found it, anyway?"

"There's no need of your trying to lie your way out of this, for we have the goods on you, and we know you're the one who attacked Mrs. Brantford and stabbed her."

"You can't know it, because I didn't do it, and you can't prove it."

"We already have proof you're guilty, so it'll go a lot easier for you if you make a full confession."

"There ain't no use tryin' to trap me that way. I've read too many detective books and comic books to be tricked into confessing something I didn't do."

"It's useless for you to deny your guilt, because during the struggle that took place, Mrs. Brantford pulled a few strands of hair from the head of her attacker. By comparison our lab specialists have absolutely proven beyond a shadow of a doubt, that hair was your hair. The one who stabbed Mrs. Brantford was none other than yourself. Why did you do it, Gary?"

Looking down at the floor, Gary swallowed nervously and his face became flushed. He couldn't escape his guilt, for too much evidence had accumulated against him. It was useless for him to deny the crime. He began to cry. "What're you gonna do to me?"

"That'll be up to the judge to decide, however, if you co-operate, the court may show you clemency. Would you like to tell us why you attacked Mrs. Brantford?"

The well of his conscience had been dammed up for so many weeks, the flood waters of guilt began to pour forth, and he had to have some relief from his sense of guilt which was more than he could bear.

"I didn't mean to attack Mrs. Brantford; I was after Charlene. She snubbed me and gave me the cold shoulder."

"Who is Charlene?"

"Reverend Brantford's daughter. I'd made up my mind to have her, and, then, that Dick Holland stepped in and took her away from me. I'd have fixed him that night of the hayride if the other kids hadn't interfered. She turned me down flat, and nobody can treat me like that and get away with it, so I decided I'd fix her.

"Besides that, accordin' to what my ma is saying to everyone around, that preacher has it coming to him, anyway. No one can treat my ma like that and get away with it.

"When I heard the preacher had left town and was gone for two weeks, I decided that was my chance, so after ma and pa went to sleep, I sneaked outa the house, walked down the road, and broke into the Brantford house through the basement window. Then, I sneaked upstairs as quietly as I could, but Mrs. Brantford must've woke up because she lit into me like a tiger. She may be a small woman, but she sure can fight. I never really meant to stab her, but I had to in self defense. It was the only way I could get outa there without bein' caught."

"Will you sign that statement, Gary?"

"I ain't signing nothin'."

"It might go a lot easier for you, Gary, if you do, and I would advise you to plead guilty."

"I didn't mean to do nothin'. What's more, my ma'll get me outa this fix; she always has before."

"I'm afraid your ma won't be able to help you this time. You're strictly on your own, for you've done something you'll have to answer for, yourself."

Gary would not yield. He remained defiant and unrepentant and would sign no statement. Finally, they locked him up for the night and kept him in jail until the district attorney could press charges against him at the grand jury hearing.

CHAPTER 21

When Rex Brantford called at the jail and requested the privilege of talking with Gary Streetland, the sergeant looked extremely puzzled.

"Reverend Brantford, as a minister you have the right to talk to anyone, and we wouldn't refuse your request. However, under the particular circumstances, I wonder if it is advisable for you to talk with Gary? I'm afraid that when his attorney hears that you've talked with him, he'll interpret your visit as an unfair advantage in the case."

"Who is his attorney, if I may ask?"

"He has no attorney as yet. If he doesn't hire one, the judge will appoint one at the time of his arraignment."

"Sergeant, I promised his mother I'd talk with him, and, as his pastor, it's my duty to do so. I'd still like to see him."

"Very well, then. We'll grant you your request."

"Under the circumstances," Rex suggested to the sergeant, "it might be well if I could talk to Gary in your presence if it's agreeable with you."

"That's right, Reverend Brantford. That may be a good idea."

When Gary was brought into the room, Rex greeted him, "Hello, Gary."

Gary sneered and looked in the other direction. "I don't wanta talk to you."

"Gary, as your minister and pastor I would like to do whatever I can to help you."

"You don't wanta help me. You just wanta get me into more trouble so you can get even with me because you think I'm the one who hurt your wife. I didn't have nothin' to do with it, and what's more, I ain't going to tell you nothin'. My ma has been tellin' everyone the things that you've been doin' and sayin' against her, and she ain't hardly got a friend left in the church anymore because of what you're doing."

"Believe me, I do want to help you. Whether you're guilty or not guilty, even though you've harmed my wife, I still want to help you. God loves you and is ready to forgive you. So am I."

"Well, I don't need no help, and I don't intend to make up

with you, neither. I just wish I'd killed her. It would've served you right."

"Gary, God sent His Son, Jesus, to this earth to die on the cross for your sins, so He could forgive you; all you need to do, is ask God for His forgiveness. Will you?"

"No use tryin' to talk with me that way, Preacher, after all you've done."

"What have I ever done against you? Have you forgotten that I personally paid the shortage in the Sunday school funds when you were treasurer, to keep you from getting into trouble? I've never done anything against either you or your folks, though there is much that you've said against me that isn't true. In spite of all that, I forgive you, and I forgive your mother."

"I ain't asking you for nothin', only to be left alone."

"Gary, whether you want me to do so or not, I'm going to do everything I can to help you. Your imprisonment is beyond my control, for you are now in the hands of the State of Pennsylvania, and I can't interfere, but I can plead for clemency, which I will do."

Gary didn't answer.

"Gary, I want to pray with you. Will you pray with me?"

The boy still remained silent, so Rex bowed his head and prayed, "Father, You have told us to forgive our enemies, so in the name of Jesus, I do forgive Gary, and I pray that You'll forgive him, too. Heavenly Father, please help him on the day of his trial and give him courage and strength. We pray that he will receive clemency from the court. Help him to realize, oh God, that no matter what he has done, he may still change the course of his life and redeem it from ruin."

When Rex opened his eyes, he noticed that Gary was wiping a tear from the corner of his eye with his fist. His chin was quivering; he had begun to sob.

"Thank you, Reverend Brantford," Gary said as he turned away, following the guard back to the cell.

Rex patted him on the shoulder as he bid him good-by. He stood in silence as he watched Gary go back to his cell. Down in his own heart, Rex was grieved to see this boy reaping the harvest of the sin of his own mother. He thought, *Gary never would have done what he did, nor would he be where he is if his mother had truly been a Christian as she professed to be all these years.* Then he prayed, "Though she is fighting against me and trying to ruin my life and ministry, help me, somehow, to win her to Thee, O Lord."

"Thank you, Sergeant," Rex said as he turned to leave.

"That's all right, Reverend. Come back anytime. I think you've done the boy some good. Good-by now."

Any good that Rex Brantford may have accomplished in the heart of Gary Streetland was only temporary, for as soon as he returned to his cell, he wiped the tears from his eyes, put on a bold, hard-boiled expression to impress the prisoners that he was still tough.

"Hi, kid. What happened?" Gary's cell mate asked.

"Aw, that was the preacher come to see me."

"Don't let 'em bluff yuh, kid. Those guys all work with the law. They try to make a fellow turn good so he'll squeal on himself and plead guilty. Yuh didn't sing, did ya, kid?"

"Naw, 'course not. Yuh didn't think I'd fall fer that kinda stuff, did ya?"

"Boy, tha's a laff. Ho! Ho! Imagine! Just imagine! The preacher, the husband of the dame yuh stuck, comin' aroun' and tryin' to act like he's yer friend. Yeah. All he wanted to do was make yuh soft, kid. That religion stuff's the bunk anyway, kid. Yuh gotta be tough if yuh wanta git along in this here world. Sure, those guys got everything; why shouldn't they be good? But look at you, sittin' here in jail. Maybe yuh did get a little sore and stick someone, but that ain't no reason fer throwing yuh in jail, is it? Tell 'em off, kid. Tell 'em off."

Gary didn't answer, just sat glowering at the floor. *I reckon he's right,* Gary thought. *You can't trust that bunch. There's nothin' to this religion racket nohow, I guess, for if there were, my ma wouldn't of said all the things she did about the preacher. He's no friend of mine. Tryin' to make out that he wants to help me when all the time he's tryin' to cut my throat.*

The youthful tenderness that still remained in Gary's heart was dying, and hate was taking over more and more. His cell mates were fast finishing the task his mother had started, of hardening his heart. The longer Gary thought, the more bitter he became. From that moment, it seemed that the Spirit of God ceased to strive with Gary, permitting him to become a hardened criminal.

After that, Gary refused to see Reverend Brantford again and sneered at the mention of his name. He devoted his time to playing cards, telling and laughing at dirty stories, and listened attentively to the prisoners who told of their life of crime. Gary soon scorned all belief in God, scoffed at the Bible, and ridiculed the church, forgetting the little he had learned about God when he attended Sunday school.

CHAPTER 22

"Rex, would you do me a big favor?" Blanche asked.

"Sure. What?"

"I've been thinking about these children who live around here. Most of them have never had a Christmas in their entire lifetime — not even a Christmas tree, though their fathers could cut down a spruce or hemlock back of the house, but they're too lazy, or else they're too indifferent. They've never been given so much as a toy, and most of them are poorly clothed."

"If you're thinking about playing Santa Claus," Rex interrupted, "just forget it. You're in no shape for that sort of thing and you know it. That's about all it would take to finish you off, and I'm not going to allow it."

"Please, Rex. All I want you to do is drive me to their houses; I'll do the rest."

"Yes, I guessed that. No. You're too weak."

"It won't hurt me. I simply can't enjoy Christmas if I know there are children who are without food, clothing and forgotten while we celebrate the birthday of our Lord with the exchange of gifts. The very spirit of Christmas is doing good, and I'm sure the Lord will give me extra strength to do this service for Him on His birthday. Why, most of these poor kids dread the very thought of Christmas, because all it means to them is a drunken father and mother who beat them while they go hungry."

"If you think you are capable of doing it, go ahead, but mind you, I don't have time to drive you around all day."

"What about Dick Holland? Why couldn't he and Charlene go with me?"

"They're in school until Friday noon."

"We'll go Saturday, then. You wouldn't mind, would you?"

"No, not if you'll promise to quit as soon as you find yourself becoming tired."

Blanche kissed him and said, "I knew you would agree. It just isn't right to forget those children and allow another Christmas to go by without letting them know the joy that comes from the birth of Christ."

"Where'll you get the gifts and things to give them?" Rex asked.

"Leave that to me," she replied. "I'll write to some of our friends in Philadelphia and have them send some of their discarded clothes and whatever contributions they wish."

Blanche was very busy the next few days, writing letters to old friends, and when the boxes began to arrive, she opened them with more joy than she would have opened her own Christmas packages.

"Just look at these little dresses and shoes!" she exclaimed. "Just what I expected, some of them have hardly been worn. They would have been thrown away or sold at some rummage sale for a ridiculous price if I hadn't latched onto them for the Lord. Some of those folks have more money than sense; they wear clothes a few times and think they are old."

Enough cash contributions were received to make it possible for Blanche to buy buckets of candy, mixed nuts and oranges from a store which sold them to her at wholesale prices. A Sunday school publishing house contributed Christmas candy boxes without cost. Friday night before Christmas, which was the following Monday, Blanche called a group of women together and directed them as they packed each candy box and sorted out toys which had been sent from Philadelphia.

"We'll have to make more than one trip to deliver all this," Blanche mused as she looked at the huge pile of toys, clothes and boxes of candy stored in the basement of the church.

Saturday morning was bitter and cold. It had snowed all night, and the crisp mica-like flakes of snow sparkled in the bright sunlight which followed the storm. The air was clear and dry, and the tires of the station wagon crunched through the snow. The giant hemlocks and scrubby pines nestled among the majestic spruce trees, reminded Blanche of sophisticated ladies going to the opera, dressed in their most beautiful gowns, wearing snow white ermine capes. *The people in the mountains may be poor,* she thought, *but they live in an environment of beauty which the wealthiest king in the world couldn't afford.*

Blanche looked twice before she saw the first house where Dick stopped. "Don't tell me people live in that tent in this country with the temperatures of ten below zero?" Blanche exclaimed. When ten children came dashing from the tent house, her skepticism was abolished. One wore a white, cotton, summer coat; the others wore no more outer clothing than stocking caps.

"Mrs. Brantford!" they screamed in ecstasy. "Have you come to see us?"

"Indeed, I have," she answered. "Better yet, I've come to bring you some Christmas gifts."

Blanche, Charlene and Dick all sat on the front seat, for the entire back of the station wagon was loaded with toys, clothes and candy. "Dick," she said, "get the sled out of the back of the wagon; and Charlene, you get some dolls for the girls. I'll get the candy and oranges."

When they reached the door of the tent house, the mother met them. She hesitated, then said, "We ain't got much of a house to invite you into, Mrs. Brantford, but I reckon you can come in if you don't look around too much."

"Home sweet home is always acceptable," Blanche answered affably and smiled cheerily. "I'll not stay long; we've come to bring a little Christmas cheer for the family in celebration of the birth of our Saviour, the Lord Jesus Christ, who came to die for our sins and to save us."

Blanche decided there was not an over supply of clothes and toys when she began outfitting these children.

"And here's a coat for you," she said to the mother.

The bedraggled mother burst into tears and said, "I've never had anything given to me. I just can't figure why you should do this for us."

"It's in Jesus' name. I hope you have a very merry Christmas, and I want you to come to the church tomorrow and enjoy the special Christmas program."

The father, who had begun his Christmas celebration early, staggered to his feet and growled, "We ain't religious, and we ain't got no clothes to wear to church."

"I think I have a suit in the car that would just fit you," Blanche said. "How about it? Do you think you could be induced to come to church if we give you a suit of clothes?"

His bleary eyes brightened and he smiled, "Wal, now, I reckon we might, being as you're so good to us."

"Good! Dick, go get that suit of clothes, and an extra orange and some candy for dad. We're going to fix him up with Christmas spirit, too."

Dick murmured under his breath, "He's already fixed up with Christmas spirits."

When Blanche handed the suit to him, he became almost childish, grinned and chuckled like an eight-year-old. "Wal now, that's shore mighty nice. You'll see us tomorry."

"Good," Blanche said. "I want these girls in my Sunday school class."

"Yeahhh!" they cried with joy and jumped up and down. "We've been wanting to go to Sunday school."

As the car pulled away, Blanche said, "Doesn't that make you feel good, when you can make a family like that happy?"

"Sure does," Dick said.

"Only you look tired, Mother," Charlene said. "Remember what you promised dad; you said you'd quit if you got tired."

"Oh my! We've just started," Blanche said. "We're having too much fun to quit."

When they arrived at the next house, a mangy old shepherd dog greeted them with growls on one end and a wagging tail on the other, and the people acted much the same. Blanche found a little baby in that house, so she told Charlene, "Go to the station wagon and bring those plastic butterflies which can be hung on the crib for the baby to watch. And bring a baseball for this little boy, and a doll for the little sister. And Dick, bring a box of candy and an orange for each one. And bring in that green dress hanging by the rear door of the wagon; I think it will fit Mrs. Jacobs perfectly."

Mrs. Jacobs, a woman of not more than thirty-five, was thrilled, and the children were about as happy as they could be when they received their toys and some clothes, too.

As they were leaving, Blanche smiled and said, "I hope you'll all come to Sunday school tomorrow."

"I don't think the mister will allow it," Mrs. Jacobs replied.

"And why not? We'd just love to have you, and I know the children would enjoy it."

"I know, but after what we heard about your husband trying to kill Gary Streetland, and putting him in jail, Mister ain't very pleased about it. Maggie's a friend of ours, and she's been here; in fact, she's been all up and down the valley, and told how your husband is treating her and the boy, and how he's tried to throw them out of the church. We figure a church ain't the place for them kind of actions; it oughta be where love is shown, not hate."

"You don't believe that, do you, Mrs. Jacobs?" Blanche asked.

"I don't reckon as how Maggie would lie, would she? I've known her a long time, and she ain't never lied to me before now."

"It simply is not true," Blanche said with a bleeding heart. Recognizing the futility of trying to counteract the wicked, lying tongue of Maggie, she left.

All day, Blanche continued to spread Christmas cheer, distributing toys, clothes, and candy to needy homes, and wherever she went, she met gossip. It was so untrue, so cruel and unfair. The joy she would have experienced as a messenger of peace was neutralized by ruthless gossip. The task did not tire her as much as the grief, and by the time she reached home, she was in tears, too weary to control her inner feelings of sorrow. She almost stumbled into the front door.

"Blanche!" Rex exclaimed. "You promised me you wouldn't overdo it! You look as pale as death. Why didn't you quit and come home sooner?"

"It's not the work that tired me," Blanche said, "but the gossip. Maggie has spread her venom all over the mountain, and we'll never be able to counteract it. Oh, Rex, we're ruined, and there isn't anything we can do about it. People believe what she has said no matter how much I deny it. It's absolutely hopeless."

Blanche sank onto the davenport and lay as motionless as a corpse. Rex was alarmed and hurried to the medicine cabinet and brought her a stimulant. As he gave the medicine to her, he murmured, "Why did you do it? Why did you do it?"

Blanche was unable to go to church the following morning. Doctor Holliday came and gave her some medicine to force her to rest after scolding her for attempting to do more than she was physically able to do. "This is serious business," he warned, "and I advise you to use better judgment in the future."

"It's not the work, Doctor, it's the gossip about my Rex; it's killing me. I just can't take it; guess I'm too weak."

Blanche forced herself to get up that evening, to place a few gifts she had purchased for Rex and Charlene under the tree. Then she went back to bed.

The following day, she arose and tried to share in the exchange of Christmas gifts, but she was pale and weak. Her usual smile was faded and gone, and she seemed to be far away. Later that morning, she dressed and cooked Christmas dinner, for Charlene had asked Dick to be their guest.

The dinner was as tasty as usual. They ate heartily, and Blanche tried to be herself, but Rex saw it was taking a toll of her strength, so after dinner, he sent her to bed while he washed the dishes.

Rex bit his lip and thought, *That Maggie is a devil. She'll kill Blanche yet with her wicked, barbed tongue.*

That night, after the Christmas celebration was over, neither

Rex nor Blanche could sleep. They lay in bed and discussed the hopelessness of their situation.

Blanche said, "I had no idea how far-reaching Maggie Street-land's campaign against you has been. Everywhere I went, the people knew the accusations she has made. She has besmirched your character and reputation to the point where the effectiveness of your ministry is curtailed."

"I know it," Rex answered. "Three families wrote this week asking for letters of dismissal. It seems that as fast as I build up the church, she tears it down. We are getting absolutely nowhere."

"The worst of it is that people have lost faith in your ministry. Many who are lost and without Christ, going into a hopeless eternity without salvation, will never be saved because of this hindrance."

"I don't see any way out," Rex confessed. "The situation seems entirely hopeless. Sometimes I think I should leave so that someone else may come and pastor these people, for I'm of no value to them anymore. This experience has so disillusioned me, sometimes I feel like leaving the ministry entirely, but then the thought comes to me, Jesus was rejected of men and crucified. He didn't quit, but endured even to the point of death. If I am to be worthy of the name that I bear, that of a Christian, I can't give up the fight for righteousness."

"Yes, if you were to give up the fight for God and leave the ministry, you'd lose your crown and hang your head in shame at the judgment."

"Right. I know that. Furthermore, I'm no coward. I'll fight to the finish, but I must confess that, humanly speaking, we are defeated. I can't see any way out of this tangled mess. If it continues my health will break, and so will yours. My reputation will be ruined to such an extent I'll be forced to leave the ministry. When I gave myself to God to serve Him I never dreamed that a so-called Christian would try to wreck and ruin my life and ministry. Tell me, why?"

"I can't understand it, either. One thing is certain, however, we can't leave, no matter how hopeless the situation may be. We must stay with the church, or we have acknowledged defeat not only here, but forever." Blanche wiped the tears from her eyes.

"I can't see the way out. The path is dark and I don't know what to do, but God does. If what we preach is true, and it is, then the Lord will show us. We must have the courage necessary to fulfill God's will, once He reveals it to us. God cannot be defeated, no, not even by Maggie Streetland, for He is more powerful than any person or any problem."

"I feel so sorry for the Streetlands," Blanche said. "Think of it, honey. Christmas must have been a terrible day for them with Gary absent from the family circle, sitting in jail. I wonder if little Sonny had any Christmas?"

"I heard they gave him a few toys. But they had no Christmas tree or dinner. It must have been a sad day. Think of it. Christmas, a sad day!"

"Yes, the worst part of this whole mess is the tragedy of what has happened to Gary. Oh, where will it end? How many innocent people will yet be hurt? Oh, God," Blanche breathed a prayer, "please show us what to do. So many people are being led astray. Satan must not win a complete victory."

"Good night, dear. Do try to get some sleep. I love you."

"Good night," Blanche answered. "Just remember that somehow God will show us the way out."

They both fell asleep praying for God's answer to their seemingly hopeless problem.

CHAPTER 23

"WHY SO MOROSE?" BLANCHE ASKED REX AS THEY were eating their dessert. It was the first Wednesday night of January, the night of the annual business meeting of the Radford Community Church, a date set according to constitutional order, and they would soon be leaving to go to church.

"Oh, I hate business meetings more than anything else I'm required to do. I wish it were over."

"I wouldn't worry about it," Blanche said. "It may turn out to be a very pleasant experience, listening to the reports of all the committees and officers of the church; it could be like a revival and a cause for rejoicing."

"It could be, yes, but it's not likely to be," Rex shook his head woefully.

Blanche smiled teasingly and patted him on the cheek as she arose to scrape the dishes, "Cheer up! It may not be as bad as you expect."

"Mom, do I have to go?" Charlene asked.

"I think you should, don't you agree, Rex? Your presence might be important."

"Yes," Rex agreed, "I think it's your Christian duty to go, Charlene. Probably there won't be many there; most generally business meetings are poorly attended."

Rex checked his briefcase to make sure he had the ballots, the membership book, a copy of the constitution, and the pastoral letter. As he clicked the briefcase shut, he said, "I've a strange feeling that something ominous is about to happen."

"You have a feeling? That's a woman's prerogative, not a man's," Blanche said, laughingly.

"Well, hurry up, anyway. Let's go," he said as he paced back and forth impatiently.

"I'm working as fast as I can. Why don't you get a dish towel and help dry the dishes? That'll do more good than wearing out your shoe leather."

Rex grabbed a towel, but his thoughts were far away, and he dropped one of Blanche's favorite dessert dishes.

"That'll be enough," she said. "We'll finish up while you get the car started and warmed up."

The journey to the church was made in silence, and Rex almost passed by the church without seeing it, and he would have if another car hadn't forced him to stop while it parked.

"You aren't paying much attention to your driving, are you, Rex?" Blanche chided.

"To be honest, no, I'm not. In fact, I was jolted when I saw that we were here. I wish this were over."

"And when it's over, you may wish it hadn't started," Blanche laughed. "Cheer up! It'll all come out in the wash."

To Rex's amazement, the parking lot was filled and he was compelled to park down the road. "Looks like we may have a larger crowd than on a Sunday night," he marveled.

Rex glanced nervously at his watch, went to the front of the church and placed the membership book and constitution on the table which had been placed on the platform, then he invited Widow Hagood, the clerk, to come forward and take her place at the table.

Widow Hagood took off her plain beige coat and unwrapped the creamy white wool scarf from about her neck and head, and took her place of importance. She was loyal, outspoken and studiously quiet, generally expressing her dislikes with a grunt rather than a verbal explosion. Her maturity and insight into character demanded the respect of all people who were long since accustomed to her plain attire which was more becoming to her plump frame than lace and frills would have been.

Rex looked over the audience and was pleased to see that so many people were interested in the business of the church; there wasn't one empty seat. Conspicuously seated near the front, sat Deacon Wadsworth, arms folded and head slightly bowed in an expression of concession worthy of important characters who condescend to mix with the common rabble. Near the aisle, in the center pew, Maggie Streetland had gathered around her the six people she succeeded in enlisting as followers of her cause, because they lacked the courage to disagree with one so domineering. Among them were Mr. and Mrs. Leslie Richmond, and of course, the Gadsons would be in her corner, for they always took the side of anyone who championed a negative cause of criticism, and the other two were Mr. and Mrs. Markeel, both dependents of Maggie's, for he worked on the Streetland farm as a handyman and his wife cleaned house for her on Fridays.

Rex was almost amused until he took a more careful look at Maggie, who sat with her arms folded, her chin raised high, her mouth set tight, and her eyes sternly staring at him as if she were waiting for the final kill. *She looks like a hawk, ready to swoop down upon her prey,* he thought. *Her expression forebodes no good.*

Rex struck the table with his gavel just once to call the meeting to order. "We shall open our meeting with the reading of the Scriptures, I Corinthians, chapter 13," he said as he opened the Bible.

Deacon Wadsworth leaped to his feet and said, "Mr. Chairman, I rise to a point of order. Our constitution does not call for the reading of the Scriptures and . . ."

"The gentleman is out of order," Rex said, "inasmuch as he has not been recognized by the chair; furthermore, the reading of the Bible is always in order and no constitutional ruling is necessary. Therefore we will continue with the reading of the Scriptures."

The deacon sat and sulked while Rex read the passage and then led in prayer.

"We will now have the reading of the minutes by our church clerk," Rex nodded to Mrs. Hagood.

She arose deliberately and read slowly the handwritten minutes which were concise and accurate. One thing impressed Rex as he heard the minutes of the previous annual meeting, and that was that Deacon Wadsworth had made all the motions and monopolized the entire meeting.

"Are there any corrections of the minutes as read?" Rex asked. "If not, I . . ."

"Mr. Chairman," Deacon Wadsworth said, waiting this time for recognition from the chair.

"Deacon Wadsworth," Rex acknowledged him.

"I think something should be done about keeping paper towels in the rest rooms. This is the duty of the janitor and half the time there isn't any . . ."

"If the deacon please, he is out of order again," Rex said. "The matter you are about to bring up would come under the order of new business, if at all. However, it would appear to me that this is a matter for the trustees and not worthy of the consideration of the entire church. Now, to return to the business at hand, the minutes as read will stand approved unless there is an addition or correction. I hear no objection, therefore I declare them approved. Now for the treasurer's report. Mr. Treasurer."

Following the treasurer's report, Rex asked, "Is there a motion to approve and express appreciation to our treasurer for a job well done, a job which required endless hours of labor?"

Deacon Wadsworth arose before anyone else could and said, "I move you we appoint a committee to go over our treasurer's books to make sure that everything is in order."

Rex was stunned. "Is there a second to this motion? I hope not," he added quickly, "for I'm sure we have no reason to question the honesty and integrity of so faithful a member of our church."

"Second," one of Deacon Wadsworth's admirers said.

There was half an hour of discussion, and finally the motion was voted down, much to Rex's relief.

"There being no more old business, we will proceed with the election of officers," Rex said. After passing out the ballots, on which appeared the names of those previously nominated by the Nominating Committee, Rex asked, "Are there any additional nominations from the floor?"

Deacon Wadsworth arose, and to Rex's amazement, he nominated the one man for treasurer whom the deacon disliked the most. Again and again he made nominations until the ballot was filled with new names, some being nominated for more than one office. *What is he up to?* Rex wondered. *Surely, he has something in mind other than being seen and heard.*

Not until the ballots had been counted and the tellers brought in the final tally did he comprehend what the deacon's scheme was. But the result made plain his purpose, for he had deliberately split the votes of those whom he didn't want in office by nominating their own close friends, so that his choice was elected by narrow margins. *So that's the way he controls the church?* Rex bit his lips.

The deacon's cleverness had another effect: disgusted people began to leave the meeting until it appeared there wouldn't be enough members left to constitute a quorum sufficient to carry on business, so Rex requested, "Please, friends, there is much important business to be transacted yet and we will need you. Stay if you can, please."

It suddenly dawned on Rex that many of his most loyal supporters had left, and there remained the deacon, Maggie Streetland and a few timid people who were easily led.

As soon as opportunity was granted to discuss new business, the deacon was on his feet again, this time gloating as a victor who has carefully fenced his opponent into a corner and is now ready for the final brilliant strike. "Mr. Chairman," he said deliberately, this time waiting for recognition as an important person would.

"Deacon Wadsworth," Rex said and swallowed.

The deacon turned around and faced the audience. "Ladies and gentlemen, what I'm about to say isn't pleasant and I wish it weren't my duty to be the spokesman, but I can't shirk my duty. What I have to say concerns the pastor himself who for some inexplicable reason has a strong feeling of antipathy toward one of our most faithful, devoted and Christ-spirited members, Mrs. Streetland, and I fear that unless an understanding is reached and an apology is made, we are in serious danger of losing her as a member of this church. Therefore, I wish to yield to Mrs. Streetland to give her opportunity to present her charges against the pastor."

Rex's face burned and his eyes snapped. Arising, he struck the table with his gavel, but before he could say a word, Maggie was on her feet and, ignoring his gavel, she began to pour out the most vicious attack possible, and Rex soon learned that she was an extremely clever and capable speaker. All truth or all error would not have been as harmful as was the truth tainted with falsehood, and she was deliberate in her misrepresentations, twisting facts into error.

"Our pastor accused my son of stealing money from the Sunday school treasury, and I'll admit there was a shortage, but not due to any error on his part, but to make Gary look guilty, he even went so far as to borrow money and apply it to the shortage in the Sunday school account."

"Mrs. Streetland," Rex interrupted angrily, but Maggie defiantly shouted, "I have the floor," and continued her tirade.

"His daughter snubbed my Gary and refused to have a date with him, going around with that good-for-nothing Dick Holland instead, and treating my son as if he were some dangerous character to be avoided. Then, when his wife was attacked, the pastor went to the police and cast suspicion upon my son by giving them the knife that Gary had lost in the snow some days before the crime was ever committed, when all the time the guilty person . . . and I have an idea who it was, for the knife was found on the corner of Holland's property . . . the guilty person, I say, found that knife and used it to attack the minister's wife and then threw it back where the preacher found it."

On and on she went. Rex decided to let her have her say, and when she was finished, he would deny her charges.

"When that accident occurred, when Danny was shot, the pastor accused my Sonny of doing the shooting, and even had the audacity to come to my house when I wasn't there and try to turn my own son against me and make him think the preacher was right and I was wrong. My Sonny didn't kill Danny, the boy accidentally shot himself.

"Now the latest, it's the worst of all, he recently had the nerve to go to jail and talk to Gary and try to get him to admit he was guilty, and he tried to trap him into saying some things in the presence of the Sergeant which would have incriminated him when he isn't guilty at all."

Maggie's speech lasted an hour. Most of Rex's friends left by the time she finally sat down, exhausted and weeping.

Deacon Wadsworth was back on his feet and said, "I yielded the floor to Mrs. Streetland, now I'll continue. Ladies and gentlemen, I think I'm serving a righteous cause by making the following motion. I move that our pastor be compelled to publicly apologize to Mrs. Streetland, and that he be forced to retract his false accusations against her son, Gary."

Rex didn't ask for a second, "Just a minute," he said, "these

charges are false and trumped up, and I deny them all. Before
you pass a motion to condemn a man, it is only fair to hear both
sides of the story. I've done nothing against either Mrs. Streetland
or her son, and I have no desire to harm either of them, even now.
Mrs. Streetland has taken facts and twisted them into falsehoods,
making them appear plausible, but I assure you they are not true.
However, I refuse to be placed in a position of self-defense, but
I do demand that you yourselves investigate into the true facts of the
case before you condemn me."

The Sunday school superintendent arose and asked for the
floor. "The chair recognizes Mr. Leighton," Rex said.

"I can testify to the facts regarding the shortage in the
Sunday school treasury. Gary did steal the money to take a trip
in an airplane, but the money was repaid. I thought Gary had
paid his own debt, but now it turns out that the pastor paid it for
him. I think he has gone more than the second mile in this case."

"Thank you," Rex said.

"I demand a vote on my motion," Deacon Wadsworth called.

"Sorry, but there was no second to that motion, Deacon,"
Rex said.

"I second it," Maggie said.

"The motion has been made and seconded," Rex said. "However, before the motion is brought to a vote, I would like to say
that no motion in this world can compel me to admit guilt when
I'm innocent. When the facts come out in Gary's court trial, you'll
know how false these charges are. Now, all in favor, please say,
aye."

"Opposed, no."

"Motion is lost."

"I move we adjourn," Mr. Leighton said.

"Is there a second?" Rex asked.

"Second."

"All in favor of adjourning, please say, aye."

"The motion is carried," Rex said, "the meeting is adjourned."

The procedure was so fast, neither Wadsworth nor Maggie
were able to stop it, for Rex gave them no opportunity to be
recognized from the floor and they didn't even vote against the
motion. As soon as the meeting was adjourned, the deacon began to shout for recognition. Calmly, Rex said, "Sorry, Deacon, this
meeting is dismissed."

"I'm glad that's over," Rex said when he was in the car. "If anyone had told me I'd live to see such a business meeting take place in a church, I wouldn't have believed him."

Blanche chuckled with amusement. "At least it was most unique," she said. "I'll warrant no other church ever had a similar business meeting."

"That's because they don't have Deacon Wadsworth and Maggie Streetland as members. They make a great combination."

"Oh, I'm sleepy," Charlene said as she yawned. "Let's hurry and go home."

"You're right," Rex agreed as he started the motor and pulled away from the church.

"Rex, do you think Maggie herself believes what she said in that meeting tonight?" Blanche asked. "Surely, she knows those things aren't true."

"I wouldn't know," Rex answered. "She's an enigma to me." After a moment of thoughtful silence, he said, "Maggie's a smart, shrewd woman, but she's also neurotic, and she may have things so mixed up in her own mind that she sincerely believes everything she said. One thing is certain, however, if she doesn't believe her own fairy tales, then she's the most unscrupulous woman I've ever met. Take your choice: she's either crazy, or else she's the world's worst liar."

"Either way, it doesn't make a nice picture, does it? and I tremble to think how this whole affair will end. Really, Rex, I'm concerned; that woman's liable to ruin you, and with the help of the deacon, encouraging her, the storm clouds are building up and becoming blacker each moment. Seems the situation is growing progressively worse, not better."

CHAPTER 24

THAT MORNING WHEN REX WAS SERVED WITH A subpoena to appear before the Grand Jury, he accepted it noncommittally, but when they served a subpoena for Blanche and Charlene also to appear, his obvious expression of disfavor brought an apology from the officer of the court. "Sorry, Reverend, but it's a matter of duty."

"Yes, I know, only it's unfortunate Mrs. Brantford must be dragged into this mess. I think she's suffered enough, and you have no idea how much hate and resentment has already been stirred up against us without our being forced to witness against Gary."

"But Reverend, if law and order is to be maintained, we must . . ."

"Yes, I know," Rex interrupted with a wave of his hand. "It's our inescapable duty, and it's something that can't be helped; it's just unfortunate, that's all. I'm not blaming you, understand, and we'll be there."

"I hated to do it," the officer explained as he walked toward his car.

"Rex, I don't want to witness against that boy," Blanche said. "That'll be the final climax to our situation here, and when Maggie hears about it, she'll twist it around and accuse us of framing Gary and sending him to jail."

"Worse yet," Rex added, "Gary will be our enemy for life, and we'll never be able to win him to Christ. I'd much rather exert my influence to save him rather than to punish him, but we have no choice; duty can't be cast aside."

Rex, Blanche and Charlene drove to the courthouse together. He assisted Blanche as she climbed the steep steps to the courthouse and to the third floor court room. She was pale and weak, and trembled when they called for her to enter the court room where the grand jury hearing was in progress.

Rex bowed his head and prayed for her as he waited, and when she finally was dismissed, she left the room, almost staggering to the door. Rex was frightened when he looked up and saw her enter the waiting room, and quickly arising, he took her arm, assisting her to a chair.

"I'm glad it's over," she said as she sank into the chair. "It did something to me to relive that horrible experience once more." Blanche began to sob.

"Now, now, just forget it if you can," Rex comforted her.

"But I dread to think of appearing again at his trial if he is indicted," she sobbed, "and he will be; I'm sure of that."

At that moment, Rex was called into the hearing and was forced to leave her.

"Reverend, you're the one who discovered this knife, I believe?" the Prosecuting Attorney asked.

"Yes, sir, I am."

"Where did you find it?"

"On the Streetland farm, near the creek."

"How did you happen to find it?"

"We were deer hunting, and I happened to see it as it reflected in the sunlight."

"Why did you suspect that it might be the knife used in the attack on your wife?"

"It was smeared with blood, and . . ."

"And what, Reverend?"

"It looked like a knife I'd seen before."

"When and where did you see it before?"

"At a young peoples' wiener roast last fall. It looked just like a knife Gary Streetland had."

"Tell us, what happened on that occasion?"

"Gary threatened Dick Holland with a knife, but the young men disarmed him."

"One other thing, Reverend, is it true that Gary stole funds from the Sunday school treasury?"

"Yes, he stole fifty dollars. I borrowed from the bank and paid it back."

"Were you compelled to deal with Gary at that time?"

"Yes, I faced Gary with the evidence I had against him, and finally forced him to admit his guilt, but he refused to make right his wrong, so I personally borrowed the money and squared the account for him to save both his reputation and to avoid a mess in the church."

"Did this antagonize Gary?"

"Yes, it did."

"Was he further antagonized when your daughter refused to associate with him?"

"I'm afraid so; he was quite possessive, and you can't exactly blame her."

"You may go; and Officer, call the daughter, Charlene, please," the Judge said.

As Rex entered the waiting room Charlene was called. When she came out of the jury room, her face was flushed and her hands tightened into a fist.

"What did they ask you, Charlene?" Blanche said.

"If Gary had ever threatened me. I had to tell them the truth; he had, just before the attack was made."

"I'm afraid Gary is in trouble, and I'm also convinced he's guilty," Rex said. "He'll likely be sent to prison for many years, and his entire life will be ruined. But more important, what will happen to his soul?"

When Rex, Blanche and Charlene returned home, before they

entered the house, they could hear the phone ringing. Rex answered it. He stood listening, but without making comment, until a frown furrowed his brow. He placed his hand over the phone and said, "It's Maggie. She's on one of her tirades, and my guess is, she'll be good for at least another hour."

Blanche shook her head and said, "That woman." She went upstairs, and went to bed. She couldn't take any more.

"But Maggie . . . Maggie . . . I didn't . . ." It was useless to even try to say anything, so Rex laid the phone on the table and removed his hat and coat. When he returned to the phone, she was still talking, crying, sobbing and at times screaming, so he again put the phone on the table and went to the kitchen and put the coffee pot on the stove and started it perking. Ever so often, he returned to the phone, listened for a moment and went about his business again. An hour later, when he picked up the phone, there was dead silence, so he asked, "Maggie, are you there?" She wasn't; she had hung up.

When Blanche came downstairs, she asked, "What did Maggie have to say?"

"I don't know. I didn't listen, but when she took off on her flight, she said she had heard that we were seen going in and out of the courthouse, and word had reached her that we were there to witness against Gary, and we were wickedly seeking to have her innocent son electrocuted for murder. She just landed at the airport again, a few moments ago, at least the engine wasn't running anymore, so I hung up the phone; evidently she had run out of gas, or breath, both, I hope."

"Let's just hope it wasn't a crash landing!" Blanche grinned.

"Looks like it was," Charlene called, "for she's at the front door now, and she looks like the wrath of heaven in the day of judgment."

There was a fierce pounding, and the door flew open under the pressure of attack, and in bolted Maggie, crying, "You wicked, wicked man, you can't make a fool of me! The very idea, you letting me talk when you weren't even listening. Well, this time you'll have to listen, whether you want to or not," and Maggie took off again on one of her long flights of verbal attack. Blanche went out the back door, for she couldn't stand any more trouble that day, but Rex sat down in an easy chair and appeared to be listening, though he didn't attempt to say a word, hoping Maggie would wear out the sooner and knowing anything he might say would be futile. One hour later, when she arose to leave, Rex tried to speak, but she screamed, "I'll not listen to you, you're such a liar and as wicked as you can be; I wouldn't soil my ears by hearing what you have to say."

The silence that settled upon the house was almost excruciatingly painful after the din of hours of battle had died down, so Rex went to the back porch and called Blanche, "You can come in now; she's gone."

"It's about time," Blanche said. "I'm almost frozen to death out here in the cold. Well, what did she have to say?"

"I wouldn't know," he answered. "What do you say we fix some supper? I'm hungry."

"I'm not," Blanche answered, but she started frying some potatoes and dropped some pork chops in the other frying pan. "I've just about had enough, and I'm ready to leave here. It isn't worth it."

"On that we agree," Rex said.

CHAPTER 25

It was early in the morning, Charlene had left for school, and Rex was anxiously waiting for delivery of the morning newspaper before he went to his office. It was one of those beautiful, false spring days, when the sun shines warmly and causes one to wish he were in Florida, and the quiet stillness seems to whisper, "This is a wonderful world; all is well and there can be no wrong."

As soon as the mailman's car pulled away, Rex hurried to get the newspaper, hoping there would be some report on the decision of the Grand Jury regarding Gary. As he returned toward the house, he opened the paper and stopped, holding it in front of him. He was shocked!

Slowly he walked to the front porch, reading as he went, stopping at the front door to read more.

Blanche opened the door and asked, "Well, what is it? What does it say?"

"Look at this!" He held the newspaper so she could see the headlines.

"Gary Streetland Indicted for Attempted Murder!" the headlines read. There was his picture on the front page, also a picture of the church, Blanche, Charlene, and Rex.

"They've made quite a story of it," Blanche commented.

"Yes, and it won't do the church any good, either," Rex said. He pointed at excerpts as he read them: " 'The crime centered about the little Radford Community Church and was committed by one of the young people . . . The pastor of the church brought charges and witnessed against one of his own young people who attempted to murder his attractive wife while he was away in a revival meeting in Olean, New York. . . . The impassioned young man was bitter because the minister's beautiful, teenage daughter had rejected him after casting him aside for another youth of the community. . . . Like many teenagers, the youth went berserk and attacked the girl of his dreams, who was unexpectedly defended by her mother, forcing the youth to protect himself by attacking her. . . . Now the youth faces a possible ten years imprisonment. . . . His pastor demands prosecution.' "

Rex threw the paper down on the table and paced the floor. "Why would a newspaper misrepresent facts like that?"

"Because they're trying to make a story out of it; it's their big chance to sell a lot of papers and get many new subscribers. After all, if a modern Romeo and Juliet romance is in progress, people won't want to miss a single copy of the paper; they'll stand and wait in line for the paper to be delivered so they can read the next chapter. I dare say, before this trial is over they'll make a hero and martyr out of poor Gary and you'll be a monster worthy of death."

"What burns me up is the fact that you were almost killed, and you suffered for weeks in the hospital with wounds inflicted by an irresponsible rascal, for whom we have done everything in our power, but we're supposed to be the ruthless, heartless creatures who are abusing this innocent, misguided victim of circumstances."

Blanche picked up the paper, sat down on the davenport and read the story more carefully, while Rex went to the kitchen and poured himself another cup of coffee. He returned to the living room with the coffee and sat down in a chair, facing Blanche.

"This is awful," she said. "Listen to this: 'The boy's mother is griefstricken and under the doctor's care.' You'd think, the way this reads, that you'd purposely tried to hurt Maggie, and the public will surely sympathize with her now."

"She'll delight in that," Rex said. "It'll feed her ego until she'll doubtless put on an act that'll beggar description."

"Rex, what a monster you are! According to this newspaper

story, 'from the day the new pastor arrived, he has opposed the Streetland family, practically forcing them to withdraw from the little church which they have faithfully attended from their youth.'"

"Great!" Rex exclaimed. "I could sue them for that, but I won't, and they know it."

"It does make a good story, however; you'll have to admit that. Say, here's something. It says that Judge Karl Winters has appointed Attorney Attwood Martin as legal counsel for the accused youth, inasmuch as the defendant is unable to hire an attorney for his family are in dire circumstances, the father having been unemployed for three years."

"Great!" Rex said. "I think I'll go and visit a bit; I've had enough!"

Blanche was still reading the paper when Rex's car roared away.

He went to the hospital first, and when he entered the front door, people looked at him curiously, shunning him, and responded coldly when he greeted them with a forced, cheerful, "Good morning." Even the sick showed their feelings by withdrawing from him and refusing to talk.

He went to see Widow Hagood, who had been ill with a gall bladder attack, and she said, "Pastor, if you're a man of God and love everyone, why don't you withdraw your charges against Gary Streetland? After all, he is just a child and you shouldn't hold a grudge against him. God is love, and therefore we should love everyone, even our enemies, and surely if you believe what I've heard you preach, you should love poor Gary, even if he did harm your wife."

"Sister Hagood, I haven't pressed charges against Gary, and I don't wish him any harm, but I can't stop the due processes of the law, for Gary has committed a crime and must face the consequences. Regardless of what I might do, the court will demand prosecution of Gary."

"That isn't what the morning paper says, Reverend, and papers don't lie. They wouldn't dare print it if it weren't true."

Rex smiled and said, "They did, and it isn't true."

"This'll hurt our church, Pastor. Don't you think for the sake of the church and the Lord, you should forgive Gary and get him out of this terrible situation? How'd you like to have your own pastor accuse you in court and send you to jail, maybe for ten years?"

"Now let's get this straight," Rex answered deliberately and emphatically. "I told you I didn't press charges against Gary, and I didn't accuse him of anything; incriminating evidence has done that, and I can't change the truth which convicted him nor undo the crime he's committed. As far as forgiving him is concerned, I already have."

"Then why is he still in jail?" the widow insisted.

"Because the State of Pennsylvania doesn't play favorites with criminals, and the law knows no mercy. I can't change that."

"I still think you could do something if you wanted to, and so does the newspaper. I feel sorry for his mother, too. Poor Maggie Streetland, her heart must be broken. Have you been to see her?"

"Do you think she'd receive me if I went?"

"I doubt it, not until you undo the wrong you've done."

Recognizing the utter futility of reasoning with Mrs. Hagood, he prayed and left.

Returning home at noon for lunch, he told Blanche, "Everywhere I went this morning I was shunned or else berated for being such a monster. People have an idea that whatever appears in print must be true. They have swallowed that story in the morning paper and I've become the number one enemy of society, on a par with Al Capone and John Dillinger."

"At last Maggie has won," she replied. "What she couldn't do with her smear campaign in weeks, the paper has accomplished in just one edition. Why don't you go and talk with Maggie and Gary, and see if you can straighten things out with them?"

"Do you think it would do any good?"

"No, it wouldn't; it'd be a big mistake to even try; I was just thinking out loud, trying to explore every possible solution to our problem, but I guess there's nothing we can do but pray."

"No matter what I do, it'll be wrong," he said. "I'll just keep busy, visiting and preaching, and leave it in the hands of the Lord. He's the only one who can straighten out this mess."

That evening was prayer meeting night at the Radford Community Church. When they arrived at the church, only three cars were parked outside. Rex said, "We must be early," and looking at his watch, added, "On the contrary, it's time to start."

"I wonder where everyone is?" Charlene asked.

"I don't know, but they're certainly not here."

"They may be a little late, but maybe they'll come," Blanche said wistfully. But they didn't. There were only twelve present that night, whereas ordinarily more than one hundred attended.

CHAPTER 26

AFTER RETURNING FROM PRAYER MEETING, BLANCHE
said, "I'll fix some sandwiches and hot chocolate so we can relax a bit before we go to bed. Why don't you and Charlene turn
on the radio and listen to it while I'm getting lunch ready? It'll
help us to forget our troubles."

"Daddy, there's a good program on the network. Shall I
get it?"

"Yes, do. What is it?"

"It's the Philharmonic Orchestra; they play nothing but clas-
sical music."

"Excellent! That'll be restful."

Rex stretched out on the davenport and Charlene threw a
blanket over him. He closed his eyes and listened with contentment to the soothing music, but suddenly the music stopped and
the announcer said, "We interrupt this program to bring you a
special news bulletin."

Rex opened his eyes and sat up.

"There has been a jail break, and six desperate criminals have
escaped from the county jail. Included among them is the recently indicted Gary Streetland who attempted to slay the wife
of a well-known minister, Reverend Rex Brantford."

Blanche ran into the dining room. "What's that? What'd he
say?"

Rex motioned for silence, and the announcer continued, "We
do not at this time have full details of the jail break, but stay
tuned to this station for further information which we will bring
to you as soon as we receive it."

The music resumed.

"What did he say about Gary?" Blanche asked.

"He's escaped jail, he and five other criminals. They gave
no details."

"Oh, Daddy, I'm scared," Charlene said. "Do you think he
might come here?"

"I hope not."

"That's terrible," Blanche said as she returned to the kitchen.
In a few minutes she returned with trays of sandwiches and
steaming hot chocolate.

As they were eating, the announcer again interrupted the program and said, "We now have additional information relative to the jail break. One guard has been slain, another has been seriously injured and isn't expected to live, and six extremely dangerous criminals are at large, armed with revolvers and rifles stolen from the police arsenal. These men are exceedingly dangerous, all killers capable of committing the most vicious crimes. Therefore we warn all citizens to keep their doors locked and don't allow anyone to enter your house unless you know them. We repeat, keep all doors at your home locked. If any suspicious characters should appear at your door, call the police immediately. Stay tuned to this spot on your dial for further announcements on the jail break."

Rex arose and hurriedly locked all the doors of the house which they normally never bothered to lock.

"Oh, Daddy, what'll we do? I'm sure he'll try to come here and get even with us," Charlene said.

"God will take care of us, my dear, so quit worrying and try trusting instead," Blanche said.

"I just wonder where that kid will go, and what he will do," Rex said.

"What if he were to come here and ask to come in. What would you do?" Blanche asked.

"Not much chance of that," Rex replied. "What concerns me is the possibility of what may happen now that he's escaped. All six of them are guilty of murder, and inasmuch as an officer has been killed, the law enforcement agencies will scour this area until they find them, and when they do, they'll show no mercy."

"At last, our bad boy has become a murderer," Blanche sighed. "It's too late to save him now; he's lost forever, and we've failed completely as far as he's concerned. It's awful, simply awful."

"Yes, and our situation becomes more involved and hopeless," Rex said.

Charlene cupped her hands on the window and looked outside. "Oh!" she cried.

"What's up?" Rex asked.

"Nothing, I guess. For a minute I thought I saw someone out there, but I guess it was just a shadow. I've got the jitters."

"Don't you think you should go to bed and get some sleep, Charlene? After all, you must get up early tomorrow and go to school," Blanche said.

"Oh, Mother, I can't sleep; I'm too scared. Besides, I won't be able to sleep one wink until I know what's happened."

They didn't have long to wait before another announcement came over the radio: "We now have complete information on the jailbreak story. A person dressed like a minister went to the county jail and requested the privilege of visiting Gary Streetland, claiming that he was the new pastor of the Trinity Church. Whereupon the desk sergeant called one of the deputies who took the key and accompanied the minister upstairs to the cell block where Gary was incarcerated. As soon as the door was unlocked, the man posing as a minister struck the deputy on the head with a black jack which he had in his pocket, knocking him out, and grabbing the keys, he unlocked the cells which housed the six desperate criminals and set them free.

"As the criminals fled downstairs, the minister drew a revolver from inside his Bible which had been cut out to hide the weapon, and shot the sergeant, killing him instantly, whereupon they raided the arsenal, arming themselves with revolvers and rifles.

"They fled in a car which awaited them across the street according to witnesses at the scene of the crime.

"We wish to repeat, these men are all dangerous criminals and armed; they will kill and are hiding somewhere in this area. Do not attempt to capture them, but phone the police if you should see anyone who you think is suspicious. We'll bring you further news as fast as additional information is available, so be sure to stay tuned to this station."

"Phew-w-w!" Rex sighed. "I feel like a fox being tracked down by hunters. I wish they'd catch them. They're bound to do something, and that right soon, for they haven't a cent and they are dressed in prison clothes. They'll strike like a cobra within a matter of a few minutes."

They waited in silence, not listening to the music, but for the next announcement. It came thirty minutes later. "A filling station, about ten miles east of Port Allegheny, on Route Six, has just been held up by three armed men, who bound and gagged the owner and proprietor after robbing his till of some thirty dollars. They took the keys to his car from his pocket and made their getaway in his car. State police have set up a blockade in this area, and it'll be impossible for them to escape, so they will be compelled to seek shelter in homes in this area. Therefore we urge you to be exceedingly careful."

"Br-r-r," Charlene said and went upstairs.

"I don't like this," Rex said. "I wish they'd catch that bunch before they kill someone. Did Charlene go to bed?"

"I think so; she went upstairs."

"Poor kid; she's worried."

"You can't blame her. Gary's more apt to be after her than anyone else."

CHAPTER 27

REX WAS TOO CONCERNED TO GO TO BED, SO HE LEFT the radio on and drowsily listened to the soothing music that followed until, at last, he was only half conscious. Blanche had curled up on the davenport close beside him, hoping to gain a sense of security, and had fallen fast asleep.

Rex awakened with a start! He thought he had heard something fall in the basement, but after listening intently and failing to hear anything, he closed his eyes again.

"I have a score to settle with you," a voice snarled.

Rex opened his eyes and saw Gary standing between the dining room and living room, pointing a revolver at him. Rex suddenly sat erect, poking Blanche to awaken her.

"Stand up, both of you, and face that wall," Gary ordered. "Hurry up, I ain't got all night, so let's get this over with."

"Gary, God won't allow you to harm us without punishing you, for He said, 'Whosoever shall offend one of these little ones which believe in me, it were better for him that a mill stone were hung about his neck, and that he were drowned in the depth of the sea.'"

"Shut up and move!" Gary ordered. He followed them across the room until he stood not more than ten feet behind them. "I'll give you just fifteen seconds to say your last prayer before I shoot. You said you wanted to go to heaven, and you weren't afraid to die; now we'll see."

An unexpected voice behind him said, "Drop that gun, Gary!"

He wheeled around, swinging his revolver toward the sound of the voice and found himself staring into the barrel of a .410 gauge shotgun.

"Drop it, I said, Gary." Charlene was hidden, lying on the

stairs, pointing the gun at Gary, and he knew he didn't have a chance, so he threw his revolver to the floor.

"Now, raise your hands and face that wall. Daddy, pick up his gun," Charlene said.

Rex heaved a sigh of relief and picked up the gun. "All right, Gary, you may turn around now," he said. "Sit down. I want to talk with you."

Gary glared at Rex, but he accepted his fate.

"Blanche, this lad's hungry; you and Charlene go to the kitchen and cook him some bacon and eggs and whatever else you can scrape together."

Gary looked puzzled and he opened his mouth in disbelief.

"You are hungry, aren't you, Gary?"

Gary nodded. "It ain't no use trying to talk me into givin' myself up, Reverend Brantford, because I've already made up my mind I ain't going to do it, not after killing that policeman; they'd send me to the electric chair for sure. Besides, I ain't goin' to double-cross the gang."

"If you had good sense, that's exactly what you would do, and if you did, there'd be a good chance you might get by with just a life sentence, and a pardon would always be possible after that, but I imagine you're too big a coward to do that. You'd prefer to be loyal to that gang of hoodlums you met in jail and end up getting shot by the State Police, now wouldn't you?"

Gary bit his lips and made no comment.

"That isn't what I want to talk about, however. First, I want to say, you've been running away from God for only a short while now, and already you are almost at the end of the line. The life of sin is very short, and the way of the transgressor is hard, but there's something to be dreaded more than death, namely, hell. Gary, it's time you got your heart right with God, before it's too late. Another twenty-four hours and you'll be in eternity unless you forsake the way of sin and surrender yourself to God."

"No, I ain't ready."

"Not ready? When do you think you ever will be ready? Time's running out on you, my boy, and this may be your last opportunity."

Gary shook his head.

"If you don't phone the police and tell them to come and get you, then I shall; either way you'll be caught. However, if you phone them yourself, it will go much better for you when you face trial. Who knows? You might even receive clemency from the court, and not only would your life be spared; eventually you might be pardoned, providing, of course, you change your attitude from rebellion to cooperation."

"No sale, preacher. The die's cast, and the way it is, is the way it's going to be. I've chosen to go this way and I ain't backing out now."

"Supper's ready," Blanche called. "Gary, I feel just as sorry for you as I would for my own son, and I'm glad to have the opportunity to give you something to eat."

Gary arose and went to the table. He ate ravenously and when he was finished, he said, "I can't figure you out."

"Why? What do you mean?" Rex asked.

"I try to kill you and you feed me. Don't make sense. If it'd been me, and I was in your place, I'd killed you. Are you trying to put on some act and prove to me that you believe the Bible?"

"Not an act, Gary. The Bible says, 'If thine enemy hunger, feed him,' and we take it literally but that isn't the only reason we've been kind to you. We want you to know we don't hate you, and we do forgive you."

When Gary had finished eating, Rex said, "I'm giving you one more chance to phone the police and surrender yourself."

Gary laughed. "No soap!" he said.

"Very well, then I'll have to do it," Rex said reluctantly and went to the phone. He still held Gary's gun which he laid on the phone table while he phoned. "The phone is dead!" he exclaimed as he listened and heard no dial tone.

Gary laughed again.

"So you cut the phone line before you came in here, didn't you?" Rex asked.

"I ain't dumb," Gary sneered.

At that moment, Charlene entered the dining room to get the dirty dishes and made the mistake of stepping between her father and Gary, who was quick to take advantage of the opportunity to escape, so using her as a shield, he bolted into the kitchen and out the back door into the cover of darkness.

"Charlene! Get out of my way," Rex cried, but it was too late; he was gone.

"I'm sorry, Father. I never thought he'd run away, or I wouldn't even have come into the room."

"Don't blame yourself; you meant no harm. Anyway, I'm glad he escaped, for I didn't know what to do under the circumstances; I couldn't leave him here with you women to guard while I went to Hollands' to phone for the police, and I wouldn't want to send either of you to make the call, for that'd be too dangerous at night, especially when there are murderous criminals on the loose. So it's for the best, I guess, only it may prove fatal for Gary, now that he's escaped."

"I'm glad you didn't have to turn him in," Blanche said; "Maggie would never have forgiven you if you'd been the one to apprehend him and report him to the police."

"With that I agree," Rex said. "I'm going to Hollands' and awaken them so I can use their phone to call the police and report what's happened, and I want you both to keep the doors locked and don't let anyone in the house, no matter who it might be."

"Don't you think you should go to the basement before you go and see how Gary got into the house? What's to keep him from returning?"

"That's a good idea," Rex said and hurried downstairs. "Look here!" he called. "He cut the glass on this basement window so he could unlock it and enter through it."

Blanche came downstairs. "Where did he ever get a tool to cut the glass?" she asked.

"He's working with a gang of professionals," Rex answered. "They probably had a glass cutter in the car in which they made their escape."

"What'll you do, now that the window is broken?"

"Nail some two by fours across it," he said.

Ten minutes later, he drove down the road to Hollands' and tried to arouse them, but after pounding loudly for some time and receiving no response, he decided it would be better for him to drive to the police station and personally report to them. He noticed the lights still burning at home as he passed by enroute to the police headquarters and prayed that God would protect Blanche and Charlene.

Twenty minutes later, he entered the State Police office and related his experience. The sergeant remarked, "He's probably many miles from here by now, but we'll send out a radio message and dispatch a cruiser to investigate the entire area."

"It might be wise particularly to check his home," Rex suggested. "He's still just a boy, and though he's acting tough, he's probably homesick and might head for home for one last visit before he leaves for other parts."

"That's a good suggestion, Reverend. We'll do that."

Rex left and drove home as fast as he could, for he was worried about Blanche and Charlene.

CHAPTER 28

AFTER ESCAPING FROM BRANTFORDS', GARY FLED
down the valley along the creek, traveling the path toward his
own home. When he reached the beaver dam, back of his house,
he cautiously stole under cover of darkness to the barn, where he
stood, carefully surveying the entire area to make sure no police
cars were parked in the shadows along the roadside. After satisfying himself that the area was not under police surveillance, he
moved silently to the wood shed. His dog, seeing him, began to
bark and came running.

"Sh-h-h-h-h! It's me. Keep still or you'll give me away." He
petted him and the dog whined an apology. "Nice fella," he whispered. "How've you been getting along? I've missed you, fella.
Now go back to the barn and keep quiet. Go back!"

The dog whined but obeyed, returning to the barn where he
sat in the shadows and watched his master, wondering why he was
acting so strangely.

Gary continued to approach the house as stealthily as possible, but twigs broke beneath his feet, making him thankful for
the heavy March wind which was lashing the bare trees and making
similar crackling sounds which disguised his blundering steps.

He wondered if the door to the kitchen would be locked;
most generally it wasn't.

What a break! he thought, as he turned the door knob and
the door opened. A nostalgic feeling came over him as he stepped
inside and closed the door behind him. Though he had just
eaten, he opened the refrigerator door, took out a bottle of milk and
filled a glass which he took from the cupboard, and he sat down
with a box of graham crackers for one more lunch. He had been
hungry for so long, he couldn't satiate his appetite.

The old family cat was now purring at his feet, rubbing back
and forth on Gary's legs to welcome him home, so he picked him
up and petted him. The cat turned on his motor full blast.

Putting Tab down, Gary slowly opened the swinging kitchen
door and crept into the dining room. The Streetland home was
never an example of order or neatness, and tonight it was perfectly
normal, causing him to stumble over a box in the middle of the

floor. The old, hard coal stove was blinking pink and blue, casting its shadow upon the walls and ceiling.

Over the fireplace in the living room hung Gary's prize deer head. Below it hung his deer rifle and a .45 automatic in its holster. Removing his automatic from its holster, he slipped it into his pocket, picked up an extra clip which was on the mantel and dropped it into his pocket also.

He rechecked the automatic and the extra clip to make sure they were loaded. They were.

The family Bible, which rested on the ancient marble-topped table, caught his eye, so he opened it and read a few lines of the twenty-third Psalm in the light of the moon. Next, he turned to the family register and there saw his name where his father had entered it. There was his baby picture, taken when he was six days old. Tears welled up in his eyes as he gently closed the holy Book.

He sat down in his favorite chair once again and thought of the many hours he had spent at home. His high school picture, which hung over the piano, though barely discernible, reminded him he would never graduate. *Those were happy days,* he thought to himself. *Days before I got into trouble. Days before I allowed hate to control my heart and mind.*

Quietly, Gary tiptoed up the steps. He stopped and listened. Yes, his parents were asleep, so he slowly crept to his own bedroom. He remembered how his mother taught him to kneel at that bedside and pray, "Now I lay me down to sleep, I pray the Lord my soul to keep. If I should die . . ." and he stopped right there, thought for a minute, and then prayed softly out loud, "I pray Thee, Lord, my soul to take."

The pennant was still hanging on the wall where he had left it. On the table were some Christmas presents which had never been opened, still wrapped in their Christmas wrappings with ribbon tied in bows. Obviously, his mother had saved them, hoping he would come home from prison to still enjoy them. Gary didn't have either time or heart to open them.

His hunting coat still hung in the closet, reminding him of many a happy moment in the fields with his dog and gun.

Gary tiptoed into his parents' bedroom and whispered, "Hey, Ma."

There was no answer, but the snoring stopped.

"Ma. Hey, Ma. It's me, Gary. Wake up."

"Gary! Gary!"

"Sh-h-h, Ma. Be quiet. Don't give me away."

"Gary, what're you doing here? You don't mean they set you free?"

"No, Ma, we broke jail. Sh-h-h-h. Be quiet. Somebody might be listenin' outside. Don't turn on no lights."

"Gary, you didn't! Why did you do it?" Mrs. Streetland grew hysterical and began to scream.

"Ma, Ma.' Please, keep quiet, or I'll have to leave."

At last she quieted down enough for Gary to talk to her.

"Ma, I just wanted to come an' kiss you an' tell you good-by. I wanted one more last visit home before I leave."

"Where're you going, Gary?"

"To New York."

"New York? You don't know anyone in New York, Son. How're you going to get there? They'll catch you, Gary. Why don't you go back and surrender yourself. Don't try to run away."

"Ma, it's too late to go back. I gotta keep goin'. You know, Ma, I never intended to git into the fix I'm in; I never planned it this way, but I never stopped to realize where it would all end when I first began to follow your doctrine of hate."

"What do you mean, my doctrine of hate? What're you saying?"

"I meant just exactly what I said, Ma. I want you to know before I go that you're to blame for all the trouble I'm in."

"Why, Son! How can you say such a thing?"

"Well, you might as well know the facts. Look, Ma, when I was a little boy you used to yell an' scream at me, and you were always naggin' Dad."

"But I didn't mean anything by it."

"Every Sunday we had roasted preacher for dinner until I finally had nothing but contempt for the preacher, the church and your phoney religion. If you'd practiced what you preached, I might've become a Christian, but I got fed up on hate and gossip. It's your fault I'm where I am, Ma."

"It's your Pa's fault, and that's what I told him. All these years he's been drinking and wouldn't go to church, settin' a bad example for you, and now look what's happened. If he'd gone to church regular like I did, this never would've happened."

"No, Ma, Pa had nothin' to do with it. You drove him to drink by yelling at him until he finally had no use for your religion or your church. The only way he could forgit his troubles at home was to turn to drink, but he never hurt nobody but hisself; in fact, I've never touched no liquor an' I never will because I've seen what the stuff has done to Pa, so if Pa's done anything, he's made me hate liquor."

Jake had been silent, but now he spoke up, "Gary, be careful what you say to your Ma. She feels mighty bad about you bein' in jail."

"I know, Pa, but how do you think I feel? I feel even worse'n she does. An' when Ma first started teachin' me this doctrine of hate, I soon fell fer it an' that's why I hated Reverend Brantford and his whole family."

"Yes, if it weren't for Reverend Brantford, you wouldn't be in this mess you're in," Maggie said. "He drove you to it, and he's the one who reported you and got you into trouble."

"Ma, it takes a mighty big man to take all that you've been doin' against him and not do anything back. Reverend Brantford and his family are all right; the trouble's with you."

"Why, Son! What's gotten into you all of a sudden?"

"I just came from Brantfords' house."

"Gary! You didn't . . . you didn't . . . do them any harm, did you?"

"I was gonna. I was gonna kill 'em, but Charlene stopped me. Reverend Brantford's a bigger man than me. You know what they did, Ma? They cooked the best meal I've had since I went to jail."

"Son, what's got into you, turning against your own ma?"

"I'm just tellin' facts. I ain't got long to talk and I got to get going, for the cops are after me and they'll kill me if they catch me here, because the gang I'm with killed a cop."

"What do you mean, you're in a gang?" Maggie fairly screamed.

"I had no choice about it, Ma. A gang from New York City set me free from jail, an' I either go with them, or they'll fill me fulla lead." Gary glanced at his watch. "My time's almost up."

"Oh, son, when will you be coming back?"

"I don't know, Ma. Maybe never. I hope I can come back, but I'm in this gang now an' I can't get out. If the cops catch us, it'll be curtains for all of us. They shot the guard in the stomach and split the sergeant's head with a blackjack when we made the jailbreak. Reverend Brantford told me that they announced over the radio that the guard had already died, so if they catch us, we'll burn. Now I'm gonna have to beat it outa here, and it won't be safe fer me to come back, so good-by."

Gary leaned over and kissed his mother. Sobbing, she threw

her arms around him, hugged him, and kissed him. "Oh my son, my son, my son. May God forgive me for what I've done."

"Good-by, Ma. Good-by, Dad."

Old Jake tried to keep from crying, but he couldn't. He thought, *If I had been a Christian, this wouldn't have happened.* Though Gary didn't blame him, he well knew that he could have counteracted the hypocrisy of Maggie Streetland had he been a real Christian, and Gary might have become a Christian. *But after all, it was Maggie,* Jake thought, *who kept me from becoming a Christian. I never did have any use for her religion, but I should've had enough sense to realize that no matter what Maggie is, Jesus and the Bible are all right.*

As Gary turned to leave their bedroom, Jake called him back, "Gary."

"Yes, Dad?"

"Gary, why don't you turn yourself over to the police? You can't get away. They'll shoot you if you don't."

"I can't, Dad. I tell you, we've got a murder rap hangin' over our heads now, and besides, the gang will kill me if I do that. They're waitin' on me before leaving for New York."

"Gary, I tell you, you can't make it that way. If you phone the police, you'll at least have a chance. Maybe you'll just get a life sentence, and if you're still alive, you might be pardoned some day. Please listen to me, Son."

"No, Pa. You don't seem to understand. I ain't got a chance in the world, no matter what I do. I'll just have to take my chances even though I don't have much chance either way, but if the breaks are with me, maybe I'll make good my getaway. Someday you'll hear from me, and if you don't hear, don't worry. 'By, Dad. 'By, Ma."

"Good-by," they sobbed. They followed him downstairs. Before leaving, he pulled back the curtains on the front windows and searched for any cars which might be hidden on the road. The March winds rattled the window panes and shook the leafless trees.

Slowly, he opened the front door, after kissing them just once more, and made a quick dive off the side of the porch, jumping into the bushes by the side of the house.

Suddenly, a spotlight, as brilliant as daylight, flooded the side of the house. A loud voice called out, "Stand right there, Streetland! We've got you covered and surrounded on every side.

Don't try to make a break, for if you do, I warn you, you won't have a chance in the world."

Gary was caught like a rat in a trap. He lost his head, became frantic, and did the foolish thing. He reached for the automatic in his pocket and started firing at the policemen. There was a cracking of pistols and Gary fell moaning by the side of the porch, wounded in the abdomen.

He cried out, "Don't shoot no more! Please don't shoot! You got me!"

"Then throw your revolver out on the road."

Gary did so, and one of the policemen picked it up and then went to his side. After examining him, he called, "Radio for an ambulance to come at once."

Maggie and Jake stood beside him sobbing, waiting for the ambulance to arrive.

Sonny, who had slept through Gary's visit, awakened when he heard the shooting and shouting in front of the house and ran to the window and looked out to see what had happened. The bright spot light, the policemen running toward the house, and the sound of sirens of approaching police cars frightened him. Cautiously he peeked through the front door which he held slightly ajar, and then seeing his mother and father by the edge of the porch, he ventured outside.

When he saw Gary writhing on the ground and heard him groaning, he began to cry. "Gary, are you hurt?"

"Go away, Sonny, you mustn't see me," Gary said. "I'm dying."

CHAPTER 29

WHEN REX ARRIVED AT HOME, HE PARKED THE CAR in front of the house, rather than putting it in the garage, because he didn't wish to chance walking to the back door in the dark. He bounded onto the front porch, gingerly selecting the right key to the front door. Before he could unlock it, Blanche opened the door. She was nervous and excited.

"Something's happened, I'm sure, down the road. Charlene and I are both sure we heard shooting, and soon after we heard sirens; first two police cars passed, and they were followed by an ambulance. They haven't come back, either."

"Must be down at Streetlands' house," Rex said. "I'll drive down and see."

He backed the car onto the highway and the tires squealed as he turned and sped down the valley. He hadn't gone far before he saw the red flashers on top of the three police cars. An ambulance was backed up to the Streetland house. The road was blocked by a police car, torches were burning, and two policemen signaled for him to stop.

"What's happened?" he asked.

"You're too late, Preacher; we just caught Gary Streetland, that is, after a gun battle."

"Is he hurt?"

"Badly. Shot twice in the stomach. They're putting him into the ambulance now, and they plan to rush him to the hospital, but I doubt if he'll make it in time, because he's lost an awful lot of blood."

The siren of the ambulance whined, and the policeman said, "Better pull out of the way so they can get through; we'll have to move this police car, too."

The ambulance, accompanied by police escort, whizzed by, so Rex pulled back onto the road, drove to the Streetland driveway to turn around, and followed it to the hospital. As he roared back up the road, he saw Maggie just entering the house; Jake had his arm about her, trying to comfort her, and little Sonny, wide-eyed and dismayed, was looking out of the window.

I wish I could help them, Rex thought, *but I'm racing with death, and I doubt if they would wish to talk with me, anyway.*

By the time Rex reached the hospital, Gary had been taken into the X-ray room, so he waited just outside, hoping to see him before it was too late. He didn't have long to wait before Doctor Holliday emerged from the room, so he arose and inquired, "Doctor, what's the story? Will he live?"

"Not a chance in the world. One of the bullets is lodged near the backbone and we don't dare operate; he's too weak from loss of blood and shock. If you have anything to say to him, you'd better not delay. We'll be taking him to a private room shortly, and the best we can hope to do is to alleviate the pain somewhat with sedatives."

"Thanks, Doc," Rex said.

Gary was groaning from the excruciating pain when they wheeled him out of the X-ray room, for though they had already

given him sedatives, the pain was so great they didn't seem to re-
lieve the suffering very much.

Rex walked behind the cart to the elevator, and as the elevator started up, he spoke softly, "Gary, this is Rex."

Gary opened his eyes and looked up. "Oh, Pastor," he said.
He stretched his hand from beneath the covers and reached for the
minister's hand.

After gripping Gary's hand, Rex whispered, "Gary, I'm sorry.
If only you had listened to me and surrendered yourself to the
police, this wouldn't have happened. Are you ready to talk with
me now?"

"Yes . . . I don't think I'm going to make it, Pastor. . . .
please pray for me."

"I will, just as soon as we get you into your room," he answered, for the door of the elevator was opening.

As they gently removed him from the table to the bed, he
screamed with pain. "Oh . . . oh . . . oh . . . Jesus, help me," he
cried.

Tears came into Rex's eyes, for this was the first time he had
ever heard Gary cry for the Lord's help. Until now, he had been
rebellious and independent of the Lord.

The nurses and Doctor Holliday quickly checked his blood
pressure, pulse and temperature; after making sure the blood transfusion was working properly, the doctor nodded to Rex to proceed.

"Son, Jesus loves you, and He'll help you."

"Oh . . .oh . . . please pray for me . . . it hurts so much. Oh!"

"Gary, time is still running out for you; won't you pray for
yourself and ask God to forgive your sins in the name of Jesus
Christ?"

"It's . . . it's too late, now . . . after all I've done; I can't ask
God to forgive me . . . not when I'm dying."

"Yes, you can. The thief on the cross did, and Jesus forgave
him, and you aren't as sinful as he."

"How could God care anything about me after the things
I've done? That's asking too much."

"No, it isn't, 'For God so loved the world, He gave His only
begotten Son, that whosoever believeth in Him, should not perish
but have everlasting life.' He loved you enough to die for you,
therefore you may be sure He'll forgive you if you will but ask.
Won't you, Gary? It's your last chance to be saved. It's now
or never, for eternity."

"Oh God . . . please forgive me . . . I'm sorry, honest I am . . . I know I don't deserve it, but please save me and take me to heaven just like You did the thief who died on the cross with You."

The boy fell back on the pillow exhausted, and Rex held his hand in his own. As he prayed and asked the Lord to help Gary, he felt Gary's hand tighten on his and then relinquish its grasp.

The doctor nervously checked his blood pressure again and shook his head. "He's lost consciousness, and I doubt if he'll ever come out of this coma; he's losing too much blood, too fast. It's just fortunate you were able to talk to him before it was too late, Reverend."

Gary breathed more heavily as time passed, and Rex stood by his side, not leaving his bedside for one moment, until the early streaks of dawn began to seep through the window. His breathing then became short and his pulse increased speed until it was in a mad race with death, but within a few minutes it simply faded away, and the heart stopped beating, only to resume its desperate effort spasmodically for a few beats, until it eventually surrendered and gave up just as Gary, himself, had finally relinquished his spirit of rebellion in final surrender to God.

The nurse checked his eyes, hurried out of the room and returned with the house doctor, who carefully examined him to make sure there was no longer life, after which, he pulled the sheet up over his face and left the room. Rex put on his coat and picked up his hat in preparation to leave, but as he was departing, Doctor Holliday entered the room.

"Someone will have to inform the parents of his death," the doctor said, "and I suppose it would be proper and fitting for you to do so, if you wish."

"I will," Rex replied.

"It's more than passing strange that they didn't come to the hospital with him and remain by his side until he died," the doctor said. "I wonder why they didn't come?"

"I don't know," Rex replied and left.

Rex dreaded his task, and all the way home he wondered what he would say to Maggie and Jake . . . and Sonny. *What will their reaction be? Will they allow me even to enter the house to tell them? This is the first time in my ministry I've ever wished to escape a duty without performing it, but I'd grasp the slightest excuse to avoid breaking the news to the Streetlands.*

When he arrived at the Streetland home, the sun was shining brightly, and its friendly warmth belied the tragedy of the hour, saying, "All is well in the world; God is in the heaven, and His goodness is everywhere."

If it weren't for sin, all would be well in the world; that's why I hate sin so much, he thought. *It nailed Jesus to a cross, and it's been crucifying the world ever since.*

Slowly he walked to the Streetlands' front door, knocked gently and waited for an answer. The door opened and Maggie said, "Come in, Pastor. I don't suppose you'd be here if there weren't some bad news."

"I bring both good and bad news," he replied. "Gary is dead; but he is also alive! Before he died, he prayed and asked God's forgiveness, surrendering himself to Christ. If only he had done that before . . ."

"Yes, I know. Thank you, Pastor," was all that Maggie said. She bowed her head in grief and began to sob. Jake stood behind her, and didn't so much as say one word. He walked over to the window and stood there looking out with his back to Rex to hide his emotions, but his shoulders shook with sorrow and he couldn't suppress his sobs.

"Is there anything more I can do?" Rex asked.

Maggie shook her head and walked away.

"Then let's pray," he said, and after a brief word of intercession, he left.

When he reached home, he found Blanche sleeping on the davenport, but as soon as he entered the door, she sat up.

"Gary's dead," he said simply. "Before he died, he asked for God's mercy and forgiveness and, thank the Lord, he died in faith."

"Does Maggie know?"

"Yes. I told her; the hardest thing I ever had to do."

"It's a wonder she would talk with you."

"She didn't; just thanked me and began sobbing. Not another word after that. It was strange; I thought she would go all to pieces and scream and wail, or even attack me when she heard that he was dead, but she didn't for some reason unknown to me. She just didn't act like Maggie, that's all."

"That is odd, isn't it? I wonder why? Do you think she was so grief-stricken the realization of what's happened hasn't yet dawned upon her?"

"Could be."

"What're you planning to do now?"

"Me? I'm going to lie down for a couple of hours and get some sleep, then I'm going to start packing."

"Packing? Why? What do you mean?"

"We can't stay here any longer, not after what's happened. It'd be much better for us to go and let some other minister move into our pulpit; he might be able to accomplish a work for God here, but my usefulness is over after what's happened. We're just the victims of circumstances and, if the Lord wants it that way, we must bow to the inevitable."

"But where will we go? You don't have another church in view, do you?"

"No, but God knows all about our dilemma."

"Don't you want something to eat before you rest?" Blanche asked.

"No, I'm too tired and upset to eat. Thanks though."

When Charlene arose to go to school, her mother cautioned her to remain quiet so as not to awaken her father.

"Mother, what happened last night after I went to bed?" she asked. "Did they catch Gary?"

"He's dead."

"Oh, no! Then he's lost, isn't he, Mother?"

"No, Charlene. Your father was able to talk with him before he died, and he accepted Christ as his Saviour." She didn't say anything about them leaving the valley, for it would have upset the girl too much.

Charlene was silent while she ate breakfast, obviously lost in thought. "I surely do feel bad about it, Mother; I feel sort of to blame for what's happened, because if I had allowed Gary to date me, maybe he wouldn't have gotten into trouble."

"No, Charlene, you mustn't think that; Gary was bent and determined to go the wrong way, and you had no choice but to do what you did, for his wrong attitudes in life made it impossible for you to associate with him too closely without jeopardizing your own character and safety."

"Good-by, Mother," she said as she kissed her. "I suppose the kids on the bus will be talking about it, and I don't know what to say."

"They may not even know it, not yet, but regardless, just say nothing."

About ten o'clock that morning, Blanche saw the mailman stop at their box, so she put a shawl over her head and went for the mail. She stood by the mail box, glancing through the letters and magazines, and suddenly held a letter apart from the others. She hurried into the house and awakened Rex.

"What's up?" he asked.

"Here's a letter; it's embossed with the words, 'PRESIDENT'S OFFICE,' and it's from the college in Philadelphia. It must be something of importance, so I just couldn't wait to find out what it's all about."

"Well, why didn't you open it and let me sleep?" he said, taking the letter and tearing it open. "Hmmmmm. Listen to this!"

Blanche flopped herself down on the davenport beside him and looked over his shoulder as he read, "The recent death of Professor Chamberlain, head of the department of theology, requires the appointment of a worthy successor; after careful consideration of qualifications for his successor, we have concluded that you are the man best suited to take his place."

"That's of the Lord!" Rex exclaimed. "I told you He would have something else for us; He knew we had to leave here and, 'before we cried, He answered,' just like the Word of God has promised."

Blanche said nothing.

"Well, say something! Aren't you excited?"

"I don't know, Rex. I'm not too sure."

"Not sure? What do you mean, not sure? It's as plain as it could be, the Lord wants us to move from here, so He has opened a door for us. Isn't the Lord good?"

Blanche arose and went to the kitchen, followed by Rex. "Blanche, I don't understand you. I'd think you would be enthused about this."

"I'd have thought the same," she confessed, "but I'm not, for some reason. I'm not at all convinced this is the will of the Lord for our lives; otherwise, I'd rejoice. For some reason, I feel this is not an opening from the Lord, but rather from Satan, who would wish to remove us from our post of duty in the hour of defeat. When I leave a place, I like to go in victory, having fulfilled the mission God intended for us to complete, but if we leave now, nothing will have been accomplished here."

"But isn't it evident that when the Lord opens a door it is an indication He wants us to leave?"

"Not necessarily. There are two doors open."

"Two? Where is the other?"

"The door of the church where we now serve as pastor."

Rex looked at her awestruck. "Blanche, I'm leaving here. Enough is enough, and I've had more than enough. We'll never undo the damage done here, and I don't care to remain in the fire any longer; the water's getting too hot."

"Have it your way," she replied, "but I don't feel right about leaving here at all. We'll see."

"Well, while you pray more about it, I'm going to start packing," he replied, and went upstairs and put on his old clothes. He went downstairs and brought up one of the barrels, which he had not thrown away since their last move, and began to pack some of the dishes, which they normally never used except for special occasions.

Blanche, watching him, said nothing, but she didn't help.

"You don't seem to know when we're through," he said, "but I'm a realist and accept the facts whether I like them or not. I suppose you think you're an optimist, and I'm a pessimist, but I'm not; I've learned not to fight the world but to accept it as it is."

There was no reply, so he added, "When once the news of Gary's death gets around, the sooner we leave this valley the better it'll be for us, for Maggie'll go to town now, and under the circumstances, she'll have the full sympathy of the people for the first time, and we won't have a chance in the world. You had better face facts, Blanche."

There was still no reply. Blanche got out the dust rag and started dusting the furniture in the living room, while Rex continued packing dishes in the kitchen.

CHAPTER 30

AFTER PACKING THE BARREL WITH DISHES, REX next removed the pictures from the wall in the living room and dining room.

"Don't forget, we must live here for a few weeks or months yet," Blanche objected, "so I'd appreciate it if you'd keep that in mind."

"We're not staying here another week," Rex answered. "By this time next week, we'll be in Philadelphia."

"And just how do you plan to keep food on the table, pay for the moving, and pay rent on a house in Philadelphia?"

"I've figured all that out."

"I suppose, but please share the secret."

"A number of churches have previously requested me to assist them in special meetings, and I was compelled to turn them down, so now I'll drop them a line and agree to help them out."

"Oh."

"Oh, what?"

"Just oh."

Rex knelt and began rolling up the living room rug. "Give me a hand, will you? Help me on the other end, so this thing will roll up even."

Blanche dutifully knelt and assisted him.

"Do you think Streetlands will ask you to conduct Gary's funeral?" she asked.

"I'm sure they won't."

"Whom else can they get?"

"I don't know; they might try the fake preacher who assisted in the jail break."

Blanche's eyes sparkled, but soon her face grew very solemn. "I don't think this is any joking matter," she said. "Gary's death is a matter of great sorrow to me."

Rex stopped rolling the rug and arose erect, still on his knees. "I didn't mean to make light of Gary's death, but if a person didn't have a sense of humor, he'd go crazy." His eyes narrowed and he looked philosophical. "You know something?"

"What?"

"I feel altogether different, now that I know I'm leaving. All of our problems seem to be so far away and insignificant ever since they ceased to have any influence on our future welfare."

"Good. Maybe that's one way of riding through times of trouble."

"What do you mean?"

"If knowing you're leaving removes the importance of immediate, pressing problems, why not just decide to leave whenever problems become unbearable, to escape wrong, and then stay? That would be a good way to overcome all worry, for truly, eventually we will leave this earth when we die, and the things we worry about, today, will cease to be important."

Rex sat down on the floor and looked at Blanche quizzically, as if she had made a great discovery. "I think you have something," he admitted. "In fact, I could stay here now, and what Maggie does wouldn't bother me one bit."

"You plan to stay, then?"

"I didn't say that! I just said, I could, but the facts remain the same: our usefulness here is over . . . finished."

"The phone's ringing," Blanche said. "Shall I get it?"

"Yes, please. Take the message; tell them I'm not available."

Never before had Rex taken such an attitude of unconcern, but he had lost all interest in the pastorate.

"Hello, Brantfords' residence," Blanche said. "Just a moment; I'm sure he'll want to talk to you." Holding the phone lightly in her right hand, she said, "It's for you . . ."

"Why didn't you tell them I'm busy?"

"It's the undertaker. He wants to know if you are free to conduct Gary's funeral, Monday?"

Rex hesitated, frowned, finally arose and went to the phone. "Hello, this's Reverend Brantford."

He paused for a long moment, but finally promised, "Very well, Monday at two o'clock. No, you needn't come for me; I'll drive my own car. Yes, thank you."

Cradling the phone, he sighed, "Well! Can you imagine that? I never expected them to ask me to conduct the funeral. It just doesn't make sense. I can't figure it out . . . just can't, but it's so." He shook his head. "Let's get back to rolling up the rug."

The living room and dining room looked quite bare by the time the day was over, and the bedrooms were upside down, also. When Charlene came home from school, her eyes widened in amazement as she cried, "What's happened? Are you out of your minds?"

"We're leaving," Rex said bluntly.

"Leaving? Why? Where are we going?"

"Daddy has an invitation to become professor of theology in the college in Philadelphia, so he's packing. He's been packing all day except for the few minutes it took to write a letter of acceptance, and we expect to be out of here by the middle of next week."

"But my school! This is my graduation year, and I can't leave now without losing a whole semester. What's the hurry? Can't they wait for you at the college until next fall? They wouldn't want you to come now, I'm sure."

"You're right," Rex conceded. "However, the sooner we leave here the better, now that Gary is dead, for our situation will continue to grow increasingly more difficult, and it's not worth the strain and worry which we would face if we were to remain."

Charlene sank into a chair and sobbed, "I think I should count for something around here, and it'll certainly be rough on me if we leave now. Not only will I not graduate, when my

diploma is only a little more than two months away, but I'll have
to attend school at least another semester next fall in Philadelphia,
and, who knows, possibly a year."

"I know, dear," mother comforted her. "Maybe we could ar-
range for you to stay here with one of the members until you finish
school; then you could come to Philadelphia to be with us."

"After what's happened? I should say not!" Charlene ran to
her room and fell across the bed sobbing.

"Here comes Widow Hagood," Blanche announced. "Now,
what'll you tell her by way of explanation?"

"Tell her the truth. Why hide it? We'll be gone in less than
a week, anyhow."

Blanche invited the widow in, explaining, "Things are rather
torn up here, Mrs. Hagood, but you can at least find a chair.
Won't you please be seated?"

"Anyone would think you were moving, the way you have
everything torn up. What're you doing — spring house cleaning?"

"No, your first guess was right," Rex replied. "We're moving."

"Moving? Where to?"

"Philadelphia."

"Philadelphia? What for? You aren't leaving us here, I hope."

"I'm afraid so. We might as well face facts, Mrs. Hagood.
After what's happened here, I'm afraid our usefulness is finished,
so we had better move on. It'll be better for the church and for
us, too, I guess."

"That's a lot of nonsense!" the widow exclaimed. "I never
thought you would run away from trouble. I always thought
we had another apostle Paul in our midst, but I guess I was wrong,
for you're just as big a coward as the next fellow. Imagine, running away from Maggie!"

"Mrs. Hagood! It isn't that," Rex remonstrated. "It's, well,
it's just that . . ."

"Go on," she scolded him. "Just that, what? Tell the truth;
you've had enough of Maggie Streetland's gossip, and now that
Gary's dead, you figure she'll blame you and the people will believe
her and make life even more miserable for you than before.
Isn't that it?"

"Exactly! Furthermore, another man can come here and do
a good work, whereas my usefulness is ruined, and . . ."

"And what?"

"And I've been requested to head the department of theology
in the college in Philadelphia, which offers me a greater oppor-

tunity than the church here in the valley, particularly under the circumstances."

"He made up his mind to leave and started packing even before the invitation to teach came," Blanche corrected.

Rex frowned at Blanche reproachfully.

"That isn't a bigger opportunity to serve God, in my opinion," Mrs. Hagood said. "They don't need you in Philadelphia half so much as we do here. There's lots of men can teach in that college, but there's no one else to minister to us, and pastoring a flock is more important than teaching a school."

Rex was stunned by Mrs. Hagood's frankness. "Now just a minute, Sister Hagood. Who are you to say where God wants me and to judge that a teaching position is less significant than a pastorate? I disagree, strongly disagree!"

"In this case, the need determines the degree of opportunity, and this is where you're needed, and this is where God sent you. He didn't send you here to run away just short of one year, I'm sure of that. Your work's just begun."

Rex shook his head. "No, Sister Hagood, there's no use talking; you know as well as I do that I'm not wanted here — and it's no fault of mine, either — and if the people don't want me here, there's no sense in forcing myself upon them."

"I don't know what the people want; some do want you, and some don't, and how many do or don't I have no idea, but one thing I'm sure of, God wants you here, and there's never been any doubt in my mind about that. What's more if you up and try to leave here, the good Lord's going to give you the spanking of your life. You just try to go and see what happens, and don't say I didn't warn you; mind what I say."

"It's no use talking, Sister Hagood; I'm going, and that's for sure, so you might as well be prepared for my resignation to be read Sunday morning at the close of the service."

"Well, I don't know. I'm going home and pray about it, so we'll see. We'll just see. Here, take these eggs and when you eat 'em for breakfast, just remember they came from one of the members who doesn't want you to go."

"You're very kind," Blanche said. "Don't misunderstand, Mrs. Hagood, it isn't that we want to leave; we simply don't have any choice under the circumstances."

"I ain't so sure about that," the widow said frankly as she left. "Don't mind me; I'll close the door behind me."

Rex slumped in a chair. "Oh me," he sighed. "I wish I'd

never come here in the first place. This has been the worst experience in my life."

Blanche kissed him. "I love you," she whispered.

"And I love you, but that still doesn't solve our problem."

"It helps some, doesn't it?" Blanche taunted.

"Yes," he admitted.

CHAPTER 31

SUNDAY MORNING DAWNED, RAINY AND DAMP; THE
wind blew gusts of rain against the windows and water stood in
the low places in the yard.

"What a dreary day," Blanche said as she looked out of the
window. "It won't help the attendance in church one little bit."

"Just as well," Rex said. "The fewer people present, the
easier it'll be to read my resignation. I never did like resigning
from a pulpit anyhow, and I dread all the crocodile tears and hypocritical farewells, when I know the people are really delighted to
see me go.".

"I wouldn't say that," Blanche said.

"Well, I would. Listen to this," he said as he unfolded a
piece of paper which he took from his coat pocket: " 'Forasmuch
as it is no longer feasible for me to continue my pastorate with
the Radford Community Church, due to circumstances beyond
my control, which circumstances are common knowledge to all,
I therefore tender my resignation, effective . . ' "

"Are there any circumstances beyond God's control?" Blanche
asked thoughtfully. "Beyond our control, yes, but isn't it a lack of
faith to say there are circumstances which have conquered us because we could not pray through to victory?"

"I take it you're not in favor of my resignation, at least you
keep talking that way."

"You know I've never been in favor of it from the very beginning, but on the other hand, I must admit that unless God inter-
venes in our behalf, we have little choice as to whether we stay
or go; nevertheless, I hate to leave. Somehow, I have fallen in
love with these mountain people and the little church. I don't
want to leave, Rex, and I sincerely wish we could stay, forever,
yes, forever."

"Maybe it would be better just to say, 'I hereby tender my resignation, effective today.' Brief, to the point, and leaves no room for argument."

"Yes, I think it's best, but I still hope and pray you won't have to read it."

"Now, Blanche, you know that nothing in this world can change the situation. You're hoping against hope even to think that anything could possibly happen to make it possible for us to remain."

"Prayer changes things; and there's nothing impossible with God," she answered.

"Oh yes, I know, but that's merely wishful thinking and you know it."

"I'm still praying, and I don't want to go to Philadelphia and be cooped up in that big city."

Rex was disgusted. He carefully folded the paper, put it in his pocket, and went to his typewriter to type out the shorter, more pungent resignation. He planned to take both copies with him and to read whichever one seemed most suitable at the time, but he felt sure the brief note was the better of the two.

In spite of the rain, the attendance in Sunday school was unusually large, but a blanket of sadness seemed to overshadow everyone. Rex listened critically as Mr. Leighton, the Sunday school superintendent, announced the death of Gary, for he was fearful lest the blame should be placed upon him, if not directly, at least by implication.

"We were all grieved to hear of the death of one of our own Sunday school scholars, Gary Streetland," Mr. Leighton said. "Death is never pleasant, but when one of our own people dies as the result of a life of lawlessness, we are particularly remorseful, because it proves that in some way we have failed to reach him for Christ. I think each one of us, teachers and scholars alike, should examine ourselves and ask wherein we have failed."

Rex searched the faces of the people for a clue to their reaction, and to his amazement, they appeared to accept the indictment. Most of their eyes looked downcast and all were lost in serious thought.

The superintendent continued, "I think it would be most fitting if we should bow our heads in silent prayer, asking God to search our hearts and show us wherein we have lacked. Shall we do this for one minute, as a silent memorial to Gary?"

During that moment of silent prayer, Rex sensed the presence

of the Holy Spirit and felt a moving of God in their midst, but
even this, he thought, would never change the situation, making
it possible for him to remain as pastor. No, he must go; he couldn't
remain another day. He must resign this very morning and allow
another servant of the Lord to shepherd this flock, someone who
would not be objectionable, who could make a fresh start without
the handicaps he faced.

As he taught the adult classes for the last time, he felt there
was a mellowing of hearts and people seemed awakened to their
responsibilities more than ever before, which caused him to wonder if a revival were not possible. Could it be that it had required
the violent and tragic death of Gary to shake these people from
their spiritual lethargy? And were they on the brink of a great
spiritual awakening?

Despite the inclement weather, the church was filled beyond
capacity when worship began that morning, and some even stood
in the back of the church, an event previously unknown in the
history of the church.

Rex's heart palpitated when he saw Maggie Streetland enter
the church, and this time, Jake was with her! Two of the members, seated in the middle of the church, arose and offered her their
seats, which she accepted.

I wonder if she's here to make trouble? Rex questioned.

Deacon Wadsworth sat at the end of the same pew, near the
window by the outside aisle. His arms were folded and his face
seemed a little longer than usual, more resolute, and his chin more
square, his jowls more pronounced. He sighed and breathed
deeply whenever he stared unconcernedly at the ceiling, which he
did quite often, particularly as the service progressed and Rex
preached.

Naturally, people stared at Maggie out of sheer curiosity to
see how she was holding up, and to the surprise of all, she demonstrated unusual control, weeping only occasionally when the congregation joined in singing.

Rex said at the beginning of the service, following the singing of the Gloria and the morning prayer, "We were all grieved
to hear of the death of Gary Streetland, but I'm happy to announce
that he did repent and find Christ as his Saviour, just before his
death. Our deepest grief is that we were not able to help him in
time to prevent his violent death, for he could have made a true
soldier of the cross had we successfully enlisted him for Christ,
and our spirits grieve that we failed to do so, inasmuch as God

placed him under our spiritual watchcare. Nothing has ever shocked me as much as this experience, and I'm sure you feel the same. We extend our deepest sympathy to the family, and we assure them they will have the support of our prayers."

Rex was not hypocritical in what he said. He was most sincere. But he was positive Maggie didn't appreciate his tribute and words of sympathy, though she appeared to accept his condolence. *Strange,* he thought. *I can't quite comprehend what she's thinking or what she's planning.*

He purposely avoided preaching on a subject which might be interpreted as either a rebuke to the congregation, or a self defense; instead, he repeated the theme of the very first message he had preached almost one year before, the first Sunday upon his arrival to his new parish. He spoke on the theme of love, and again he chose as his text, "If thine enemy hunger, feed him."

The audience was unusually emotional, weeping at times, but Rex attributed it to the strain which all must have felt because Mrs. Hagood had informed them of his intentions to resign and leave.

He constantly watched the clock as he spoke, and felt relieved when the minute hand said, five to twelve. "I see my time is up," he said, "and though I would like to finish this message, that will never be my privilege, because . . ." he hesitated and reached into his pocket and withdrew two pieces of paper. Considering them forthrightly, he chose to read the longer version of his resignation, so he unfolded it and smoothed out the crumples and cleared his throat as he prepared to read it.

He didn't see Maggie Streetland arise, and he was startled when he heard her voice, "Pastor, may I say a word?"

"Well, uh, I was just about to . . . yes, Mrs. Streetland, you may speak if you wish."

What else could I do? he thought. *Oh well, what's the difference? I'll let her have her say and won't even bother to answer her, inasmuch as this is my last day here, anyway, and besides, my resignation will be answer enough.*

Maggie walked to the front of the church, and for a moment he thought she planned to come to the pulpit, but he decided he would not stop her, regardless. He was spared embarrassment when she stopped in front of the altar rail and turned to face the people.

"Dear ones," she began, "I wish to make a confession. My son lies in a casket at the funeral home this very moment. Yes, it was hard for me to come to church this morning . . ."

Rex didn't hear the next few words, he was too busy deducting how clever Maggie was to stir up the sympathy of the people before she attacked him, but he had definitely committed himself to a policy of no defense, for nothing was to be gained by a fight, not now — he was leaving.

His thoughts returned to Maggie when he heard her say, ". . . I have done all in my power to destroy our pastor and his good family. I have been selfish, mean, and domineering. I didn't see myself as I am until the other night when Gary came to the house and awakened us to confess that he had tried to kill the pastor and his family, the second time, but they, in return, fed him and forgave him. Yes, he admitted it was he who tried to kill Charlene originally, and he was the one who stabbed the pastor's wife, but he blamed me for it all and said that if I hadn't taught him to hate, from his youth up, he wouldn't have done what he did . . ." Maggie broke down and wept.

Rex listened intently, amazed at what she was saying. Soon she straightened up and continued to speak.

"I'm sorry," she said. "Please forgive me, but I can't help but cry. I always blamed Jake for spoiling Gary, because he was such a drunkard, but Gary said his dad had nothing to do with it; it was me, and he said I was the one who drove Jake to drink, and he'd decided long since that there wasn't anything to my religion, because I was such a hypocrite."

For a moment it seemed as if Maggie would not be able to continue; she sobbed and could no longer control herself, but finally, she tightened her fist about her handkerchief and steeled herself to finish her confession.

"It . . . was . . . when . . ." she hesitated, "when I heard the shots and hurried outside to find Gary lying in his own blood, that I awakened to my own sinfulness. There lay my own boy, dying because of my own hypocrisies; he had just said so."

Maggie straightened up. Standing erect, she bravely said, "Nothing, and no one in this whole world, could have changed me but that tragic experience — seeing my own boy dying for my wickedness — but at that very moment, my heart cried out to God for forgiveness. All the hate left me, I suddenly wanted to make right the wrongs I had done and to seek the forgiveness of our dear pastor and his family whom I have wronged and harmed so much . . ."

Maggie shook her head and put her handkerchief to her mouth and sobbed spasmodically.

". . . I would have gone to them at once and asked their forgiveness, but I decided it was my duty to do it before the entire church . . . and ask your forgiveness, too, for I've almost wrecked the entire church.

"Oh, why must God deal so harshly with us before we'll acknowledge our wrong and come back to Him? Why didn't I get right with God before He had to take Gary from me? I'm the cause of all his suffering, poor boy, and may God forgive me.

"I've been so stubborn, it took this terrible tragedy to save this church from ruin and to restore me to fellowship with my Lord.

"I presume you wonder why I didn't go to the hospital when Gary was dying, but I couldn't. I wasn't right with the Lord, and I knew I couldn't help him; furthermore, he didn't want me, because I'm the one who brought him to his ruin. It's a terrible thing to admit, but it's true, and I'm just glad that the pastor was faithful and forgiving enough to go to his bedside when he was dying and help him to get right with the Lord before he left us and went into eternity, for I can at least see him again in heaven; otherwise, I would never have seen him again, forever.

"I know I'm asking much, but for Jesus' sake, will you please forgive me?"

Turning around she looked pleadingly at Rex and said, "Pastor, I understand you came to church this morning prepared to read your resignation, but please don't do it. I've been the cause of enough trouble and sorrow, and I don't want this guilt added to my conscience. Please forgive me, and I promise to support you fully in the future if you'll but stay.

"You probably wondered why I requested you to conduct Gary's funeral, but I really wanted you and I need you."

Maggie fell on her knees at the altar. Rex stuffed the resignations back into his pocket, hurried from the rostrum and knelt beside her at the altar. Blanche immediately joined them, kneeling on the other side.

Jake, who had been listening intently, began to sob. He arose and pressed his way out of the pew, and many people thought he was preparing to leave, but when he reached the aisle, he walked toward the altar, and immediately, one of the deacons joined him as he staggered forward, not drunk, but under conviction, grief-stricken and blinded by tears. He fell to his knees and began to pray aloud, confessing his every sin.

Deacon Wadsworth sat with his arms folded, looking glum,

munching on his lower lip, and demonstrating disinterest by staring nonchalantly at the wall, too proud to confess his own wrong-
doing, but thoroughly disgusted because he had lost his battle
forever.

People began to sing spontaneously, "The Crimson Tide I
See," as others began to move toward the altar.

Charlene sat beside Dick Holland and prayed earnestly for
his salvation. She wasn't surprised when she saw he was under
deep conviction.

"Oh God," she prayed, "speak to him, for he's either coming
to Thee now or never. If he rejects this opportunity to confess
Thee, never again will he experience such a tugging at his heart,
and he'll be lost, for every obstacle which he has used to excuse
himself from becoming a Christian has been removed."

Dick was silent, motionless; then, without indicating his in-
tention, he suddenly arose and went to the altar. Determination
was in his eyes.

Rex arose and invited, "Are there others?"

Yes, others moved forward, and the altar filled with peni-
tents who sobbed and prayed as they sought the Lord.

When the Spirit of the Lord ceased moving in their midst, Rex
returned to the rostrum and said, "Now I have a confession to
make, too. I did come here prepared to read my resignation this
morning, and I held it in my hand, ready to read it, when Mrs.
Streetland came forward, but now — " he withdrew the resignations from his pocket and tore them in half — "but now, I must
stay. I doubted God. Otherwise I wouldn't have planned to resign.
My wife had more faith than I did, so please pray for me and forgive me."

Deacon Wadsworth arose, picked up his hat and coat, and
stomped out of the church. The following day he dropped over
dead on the street in Port Allegheny.